Hydrogen Sleets

Michael Warren Lucas

Acknowledgements

My thanks to Richard Jones, Mark Moellering, Kate MacLeod, Josh Peterson, and Rob Rowntree for their thoughts on earlier versions of this book. Even more thanks go to my wife Liz.

My gratitude also goes to the kind, generous, and above all, *forgiving* Peter Wemm.

By the Same Author

Immortal Clay

Kipuka Blues

Butterfly Stomp Waltz

Hydrogen Sleets

git commit murder

Nonfiction (as Michael W Lucas):

Relayd and Httpd Mastery – PAM Mastery –
FreeBSD Mastery: Advanced ZFS – FreeBSD Mastery: Specialty Filesystems –
FreeBSD Mastery: ZFS – Tarsnap Mastery –
Networking for Systems Administrators –
FreeBSD Mastery: Storage Essentials – Sudo Mastery – DNSSEC Mastery –
Absolute OpenBSD – SSH Mastery – Network Flow Analysis –
Absolute FreeBSD – Cisco Routers for the Desperate – PGP & GPG

See your favorite bookstore for more!

Prologue

Unthinkable… shapes?
Must be shapes. Couldn't be anything else.
Each motion—no flow. No thought, no sense.
Hold I together. Through brutally twisted space.
Space that rips the soul.
Plunge straight in.
Rescue. Rescue all.
Or end I trying.

1

The Montague Corporation didn't exactly cancel my vacation. They just made it boring. I was in a modest green bikini, sunbathing on a chaise of almost insubstantial molecular mesh and enjoying the Congolese rainforest resort's brilliant clear sunlight and humid tropical fug, when my datalink chirped. "Montague Human Resources for Aidan Redding."

The company had an unexpected opening for a bottom-level security position.

I could have said no. Montague considers vacation time sacred, and I had two months until my next assignment.

But a surprise opening for a security third? Two months in another universe? A universe I wouldn't get to see otherwise?

I'd grown up burning to see the universes. Yes, all infinity of them.

Even if I ignored the weeks of medical leave I'd needed to get my hand regrown, I'd had a month of actual vacation. I'd visited my parents—on their anniversary, no less. Their delighted surprise still danced in my heart, but a week in the barrio had been plenty. Any longer, and the gap between us got too uncomfortable.

And the Congolese rainforest resort would be here when I returned.

Whenever that was.

Normally, assignment to a new universe requires anything from a week to a month of classroom and physical training before you get near the Portal.

Montague wanted to send me—immediately?

I'd never heard of such a thing. Which didn't mean it didn't happen, only that it'd never happened to me. The thought that I might already have sufficient training flared through my head and just as quickly died. *Nobody* had all the training needed to enter a brand-new universe.

By the time the HR system disconnected, I was already stuffing my French-Spanish phrase book into my bag and my feet into my sandals. Before I reached the airport outside Lubumbashi, they'd sent the tickets and a quarter million words of briefing to my datalink. I swept through customs and onto the Congolese Air ballistic glider, and found myself upgraded to first class. I didn't have time for the complimentary massage or the open bar—the forty-five-minute flight back to Uruguay gave me barely enough time to snatch a few important names from the dossier and memorize the universe summary.

Meet the new universe, same as the old universe.

But thirteen billion years younger.

A Montague car met me at the airport—not an automatic, a limousine. With an actual human driver, a young man hired for charm instead of brains. I noticed the vat-leather seats and the driver's half-flirting repartee, but buried myself in the Physical Environment part of the briefing. I could learn everyone's names and the org chart later, but if this universe's natural laws said "inhale and you'll explode," I needed to know right away. The driver recognized the symptoms and he didn't seem upset.

A brand-new universe—brand-new to me, yes, but also literally a newborn. Only a few hundred million years after its Big Bang. Full of nothing but hydrogen screaming out of that primal blast, torrents of cosmic rays…

And an old-fashioned space station.

Six concentric rings spun for gravity.

Eight spokes connecting them.

A weightless bubble at the core, full of telescopes.

A million tons of metal, protected from the cosmic hurricane by carefully balanced magnetic fields, with antennas and sensors sticking out everywhere. The same magnetic fields sieved hydrogen from the void to fuel the fusion reactors powering the whole thing.

Straight out of a second millennium movie.

Humanity couldn't reach the stars, but we'd weaseled our way into deep space anyway.

Excitement fluttered my pulse all the way to the Portal.

8

2

One step between the electrodes of the Portal, and my weight plunged twenty percent.

It's not like I weigh much anyway, but the sudden weight shift set my inner ear whirling and made me wobble. I automatically grabbed for the cool aluminum handrail—not that I saw it, but there's always a handrail outside the Portal.

A petite leather-gloved hand with a grip like a bear trap seized my bicep and said "Easy, ma'am, it hits everyone that way."

"Thanks." I took a breath of fresh but metallic air to steady myself.

About the size of a subway station, the Portal chamber's aluminum ceiling arched away from me, decorated by regular lines of rivets and the occasional octagonal Montague stamp. Electronic equipment and screens lined the walls, along with boxes of cargo bound in and out. Two women in khaki stood further back, one behind a slender touchscreen console, the other with a laser rifle aimed at me.

I didn't take the rifle personally. Returning to Earth, you appeared in a sealed box. If *those* scanners detected anything harmful, you'd never know it. Montague's zeal in protecting Earth from alien universes would seem maniacal, if the risks weren't so horrific. On my first assignment, an egotistical researcher had tried to carry half a kilogram of antimatter ore back to Earth. It was harmless in its native universe, but on Earth it would have knocked South America into orbit.

The little East Asian guy holding my arm wore too much sharp cologne, the smell like a barbed-wire blanket. His uniform hung too loose over his shoulders. Sensor goggles hugged his eye sockets, presenting him with a billion details about everything they picked up. He had PERCIVAL stitched above the pocket of his khaki uniform shirt. "You okay?" His voice seemed weirdly deep from such a tiny frame.

"Yeah."

Percival's goggled gaze moved up and down my body, insultingly direct. I knew he wasn't leering, but I always felt uncomfortable with someone studying me so closely. The Portal's mathematical transformations might have altered me dangerously, or changed harmless bacteria into something nightmarish, and the goggles would show that. They also exposed my skin in a display that would make a strip joint operator envious. I made myself stand still.

After a few tense heartbeats Percival said "Clear. Welcome aboard Wemm Station, Miss Redding."

"Thanks. Where's HR?"

Percival shook his head. "Y'all don't get HR." He held out a gleaming black brand-new datalink in his gloved hand. "We have instructions to send you straight to Six. Leave your bag, we'll get it to your quarters."

"Six?" Disquiet tickled my spine. The local Human Resources person should explain the rules, introduce me to my team, and give me the tour. And the tour would presumably include where the heck this *Six* was.

"Ring Six?" Percival frowned. "How much briefing did you get, anyway?"

"They *sent* the whole thing. I had maybe half an hour to read it."

Percival tightened his lips. "Don't y'all worry, we'll get you up to speed." He jerked his hand towards the door. "Out them double doors. Turn right. Montague elevator on your right. Sixth ring. It's right by the Core, so there's no gravity. Hang onto the elevator rail as you go up, or y'all'll smack the ceiling. Tell me you at least done the free-fall training?"

You have no *idea.* "Yes."

Percival nodded. "Security First Watford's waiting for y'all."

Straight to the top? That could *not* be good. "Thanks." I plucked the palm-sized datalink from his hand. The black plastic rectangle shimmered as it sampled my DNA, then chirped, "Aidan Redding. Montague Corporation. Security Third."

"Confirm," I said.

The datalink buzzed as it sucked my personal settings out of the local datacore.

"Come by at dinner," Percival said. "I'll introduce y'all to the team."

"Thanks!" I clipped the datalink to my belt and broke into a trot towards the double doors at the far end of the room.

No introduction. No tour. Not even a map.

For the first time, I wondered why Montague had an unexpected urgent opening here in a universe that held nothing besides hydrogen and cosmic rays. Was I replacing someone? And if so—why?

3

The stark aluminum corridor could have been from any Montague facility, in any universe. Straight across from the Portal room's door, black stenciled letters declared this RING THREE. Bold arrows pointed left and right to SPOKE EIGHT and SPOKE ONE. Clear, unmistakable, industrial Montague. I found the elevators a few meters to the right, in this little bubble of the corridor. I chose the one bearing the octagonal Montague logo split across its doors. "Six," I said as the doors slid shut behind me.

My datalink answered in the cultured masculine voice I'd chosen. "The sixth ring simulates less than one percent normal gravity. Secure yourself." I gripped the cool steel handrail as the elevator climbed, the slow loss of weight making my pulse throb in my ears.

A screen on the wall shifted to display *Spoke One Ring Four*. The spicy squash and beans I'd eaten for lunch in the Congolese resort, three hours and a universe ago, seemed to drift upwards. The feeling got worse as the display flipped to *Spoke One Ring Five*.

The elevator's slow stop lifted my feet off the floor, and the rail suddenly felt very slippery in my grip. *Spoke One Ring Six*. I kept my orientation, though, holding myself steady until the doors slid open and I could glide out.

According to the sketch at the start of my dossier, Ring Six was so close to the station's axis that it had almost no centripetal gravity. The builders didn't bother giving this corridor a flat surface to pass as a floor—it was round like a coiled sausage, with textured metal rings for handholds spaced an arm's width apart all the way around. I could starfish in the middle of the tube and not touch a wall, but only barely. Pristine white plastic panels circled the tube every meter across the inner surface, diffusing soft white light across the brushed aluminum walls. Irregularly-placed round airtight hatches marred the outer edge. Omnipresent vents sucked at the air, forging freshness amidst humming lights and hidden motors. Judging from the corridor's curve, this ring had to be maybe two hundred meters in diameter.

I touched the datalink on my belt. "Which way to Watford?"

"Left," came the machine's smooth masculine reply.

I used my legs to launch myself down the corridor, guiding myself away from the walls with my hands. I only needed a few pushes down the vacant corridor to distinguish the station's low, multi-tone hum from angry shouts.

Rounding the corridor's curve, I saw a cluster of people knotted around an access tube in the inner wall. The one person in a Montague uniform looked like he might have received a gorilla gene graft, with massive shoulders and a shaggy pelt of salt-and-pepper hair that haloed his rectangular head and emphasized the bald patch atop his skull. One hand clutched an anchor ring while he raised the other, index finger upraised. That had to be Watford.

"She's on her way," Watford shouted at the man facing him as I came into view.

The man beside Watford surprised me enough that I almost collided with the wall. I'd just passed through entire crowds dressed like him a few hours ago.

He was Congolese.

"I would hope so." The tall Congolese even had the accent, part African and part French. He had his feet pressed against the outer edge of the tube and one hand pressed against the inner edge, pinning him in place. Where most men from the Congolese Federation traditionally wore kilts, he'd let weightlessness triumph over tradition and wore a blue pullover shirt trimmed in blistering yellow and billowy yellow trousers instead. I glimpsed a few people behind the African, but focused on making myself slow down without crashing into a wall or Watford.

I snatched a handgrip a couple meters behind Watford. The sudden stop yanked at my shoulder, and I had to stick my legs out to bounce off the wall. "Mister Watford," I said, sketching a salute before extending that arm to steady myself. "Aidan Redding, reporting."

Watford turned to glare at me. "About time."

I got the call two hours ago, what did you expect? "Sorry sir. Rush hour."

"So, you are ready?" the African said.

Watford turned to me. "We have a mentally unstable scientist up in the Core."

From a meter-wide opening in the inner edge of the corridor, a line of electric indigo abruptly sliced into the air and stabbed the corridor's outer edge. The electronic buzz came again, this time much closer and sharper, bringing a stink of ozone. A shriek followed it, a weird constant high-pitched tone that didn't seem to come from a human throat until it trailed off for lack of breath.

My throat clenched. A laser. Not one of those vicious construction ones, but still strong enough to bubble metal where it struck the corridor wall.

That impossibly level screech disturbed me even more than the laser, though. A person's shout should go up and down. It should quaver, not remain steady as a tuning fork.

My briefing said that this universe was exactly the same as our own, only billions of years younger. Where our universe had grown up, built a career, and pushed its kids through college, this universe was still learning to burp. Other than the rotating rings of Wemm Station, the only solid matter in this universe was a hailstorm of hydrogen, pounding out from the primordial Big Bang in a flux of magnetic fields and gravitational ripples.

But that abhuman shriek made me wonder. Was this universe *really* the same as ours?

Or had the mathematicians missed some subtle danger?

Something that could drive a human throat to make that unnaturally level cry?

As the beam faded to a glittering afterimage slashing my vision and the air stopped sizzling, Watford said "Doctor Tansi's turned a research laser down the access shaft, and blocked the other entrances."

I made myself take a deep breath. A laser that powerful would diffuse a bit as it burned through me, but would still have enough oomph to punch right through anyone behind me. But Montague wouldn't dispatch me to another universe just to have me make a suicidal charge up the access tube.

"Is the remote shutdown broken?" I said.

Watford narrowed his eyes at me. "We have a plan, Third."

I didn't let my irritation show. "Sir?"

The Congolese tsk'd and rolled his free hand over his head. "You bring someone to help me? She knows nothing."

Someone to help *him*? Who was this guy?

Watford turned his attention to the Congolese. "Station Commandant Mvouba. You asked that we bring additional help. Here she is. You will permit us the courtesy of exchanging a few words before we solve your little problem."

Mvouba frowned and pulled his arm back in. "Very well."

Watford turned to me, his face twitching with tightly suppressed anger. "Commandant Mvouba is a representative of the Congolese Federation. He's responsible for Wemm Station."

I clamped my teeth together to hide my surprise. The Congolese Federation ran this station? I hadn't heard of facilities in any universe being run by anyone other than Montague.

"Montague is kindly assisting the Federation with this issue."

"Montague is responsible for threats to station integrity," Mvouba snapped. "We handle personnel security. Once you have secured the threat, we will take care of Doctor Tansi."

"Yes, sir," I said.

"Redding!" Watford's scowl deepened. "Anything you have to say to Station Commandant Mvouba, you may address to me."

A territorial pissing match? Oh, joy.

I stilled my face. "Yes, sir. Your instructions, sir?"

Watford's scowl didn't soften any. "Your file says you've had freefall hand-to-hand training."

"Just the intro," I said.

Watford's eyebrow twitched.

"Sir," I added.

The corners of Watford's mouth turned even further down. "Four whole hours, eh? It'll have to do. The plan is, Miss Redding, we charge the laser."

My formal face dissolved.

"Palmer has point," Watford said. "I'm second. You take tail. Palmer grabs the laser. You and I secure the perpetrator and hand him over to the commandant's people."

Another blast from the laser scorched the air, the buzz shredding conversation. Tansi's abhuman monotone cry echoed down after it.

"Sir?" I tried to sound confident. "We're… cutting the power first?"

"Impossible," Mvouba snapped. "That would disrupt research that has run for months now. We spent four years building this station. This first group of experiments is highly important."

"The Congolese engineers wired the lasers into the main power," Watford said. "Nobody thought that they *might* need to remotely shut them down individually."

I repressed a flinch. Montague wouldn't make a mistake like that.

Just what sort of people had designed this station?

I scrabbled through my memory of the hastily-skimmed dossier. The access tube up to the spherical Core was what, twenty meters long? No, it had to be more like eighty. The two laser shots had been maybe twenty seconds apart. Four meters per second in zero gravity, through a fairly narrow access tunnel? Almost doable, if everything went perfectly.

But there was a good chance we'd get cooked.

Maybe this Palmer person wore ablative armor that would absorb the laser's heat and burn off. Or a portable diffraction array—no, that would scramble a whole bunch of the research Mvouba was so worried about. Montague had tools and equipment for coping with lasers.

If I'd been here for more than ten minutes, or if I'd had time to read the dossier, I'd know about that equipment.

Watford studied me for a second. "Palmer!"

Behind Commandant Mvouba, someone said "Yes, sir."

"Are you ready?" Watford said.

"Yes, sir," the voice said.

Watford glared at Mvouba. "If you'll let us get to the access tunnel. Commandant."

Mvouba raised his chin and levered himself to the side, letting me take his place.

A cluster of people hung in the corridor on the opposite side of the access tube, out of the line of laser fire. The man in front wasn't carrying a diffraction array or wearing ablative armor. He wasn't wearing… much of anything. Maybe fifteen centimeters taller than me, his mid-calf pants and short-sleeve shirt were a skintight mesh of loose-woven wire-thin plastic, exposing lean muscles, well, *everywhere*. Beneath the mesh he wore only tight briefs barely large enough to qualify as a banana hammock. He had a broad, cheerful face, with cedar skin and weirdly regular freckles. The freckles didn't just cover his cheeks—they continued down his chin and up over his bald head.

Palmer didn't even have eyebrows—just the freckles.

The laser was going to fry him like a blowtorch through butter.

Palmer grinned and raised a hand in greeting. The same freckles covered his palms and fingers, all spaced maybe half a centimeter apart.

Wait—those weren't freckles.

They were sensors.

Palmer was a cyborg.

No, not the usual Earth *I have an implant so I don't carry a datalink* sort of thing.

More of the "gobs of high tech crammed under my skin" type.

Maybe charging the laser *wasn't* completely insane.

And he probably had a really good reason for the stupid outfit.

"Welcome to Wemm Station, Miss Redding," Palmer said. "Bear Palmer, Security Second."

Watford's glare and the adrenaline thrumming in my veins made me want to shout, but I kept my voice low and said "Pleasure to meet you, Mister Palmer."

"Babble later," Watford stage-whispered. "After the next blast, go."

I tried to control my breathing and slow my hammering heart.

Indigo light sliced the air, close enough to touch.

It had barely vanished when Palmer launched himself up the access tube.

4

I hauled myself up the aluminum access tube hand over hand, letting my feet dangle behind me, a gentle breeze from the air handlers at my back. The tube was wide enough that I didn't have to worry about knocking my head against the far side, but narrow enough that nobody could climb next to me. Not at the speed we hurtled ourselves upwards, at least.

We had seconds to make the weightless climb to the Core before Doctor Tansi fired the laser again. Maybe point man Palmer was a cyborg, equipped to survive a metal-melting beam of light. That didn't mean Watford and I would escape unscathed.

The next time Human Resources sent me an apple, I'd check it for worms.

Watford's boots kicked the air right above my head, so close that more than once I had to yank on a handhold to a stop myself a smidgeon of a second before I smacked his boot with my head. The stench of ozone and hot metal, with undertones of sweat and leather, filled each desperate breath.

Security First Watford had maybe sixty kilos on me. Most of that weight was muscle, true, but the truth was, even without his extra twenty years I was faster than him. I could scuttle through this tube faster than he ever could.

If he'd just get out of my way.

Forty meters up. Another forty to go. And Watford was already huffing for air. How had that guy passed the Montague physicals?

Around Watford's flailing feet and desperately snatching hands, I glimpsed the tube receding into the Core, a small disk of light marking the end of the tunnel. Palmer was most of the way up, ahead of us. Other than his exhibitionist mesh clothing and those ridiculous briefs, Palmer had seemed decent. I didn't want him facing a violent scientist with a metal-melting laser alone.

And Watford was slowing me down.

Way down.

I itched to shove past him, but that would only slow us both down. From the few moments we'd had, I suspected he'd explode at me for even suggesting it.

I clutched the handgrip ring more tightly, and fought to keep my speed slow enough for Watford.

How long had it been? Ten seconds? Fifteen?

Best case, Palmer escaped the access tunnel before the next laser blast. But at Watford's speed, he sure couldn't.

And if Watford couldn't, I wouldn't either.

I wanted to squeeze into the space between two rows of handgrip rings. Leave the space in the center of the access tube clear. Let the laser blast past me, let it take another stab at the Ring Six outer wall. Take this mad dash in two stages.

My ears strained to hear over Watford's heavy breathing, our hands bouncing off metal walls, the constant low hum of Wemm Station's air handlers. My frustrated pulse throbbed in my temples.

Watford had said there was a plan.

I had to trust him.

How many seconds did we have?

Maybe two-thirds of the way up.

A rung slipped in my sweaty grip.

Tansi screeched again, that same bizarrely constant perfect pitch. If I'd brought a wineglass it would have shattered.

Palmer said loudly "Take it easy, Doctor Tansi. Nobody's going to hurt you."

An electronic buzz filled my ears.

I couldn't help throwing myself against the side of the access tube, even though it was too late—the laser would have burned right through me before the sound arrived, before my nerves could register the shock.

No laser beam assaulted us.

The circle of light at the end of the access tube actually darkened, as if something had blocked most of the light.

Watford froze in place, hand on a ring.

My inertia carried me up an arm length, so that I found myself staring at the back of Watford's knees before I could catch myself.

Seconds later the electronic buzz stopped. The end of the access tube turned light again.

Watford jerked forward, launching himself forward like he'd been jabbed with two-twenty volts. His panting slowed into deep, heaving breaths, and he rocketed up towards the end of the tunnel.

I grabbed a handhold and threw myself after him, emerging into the spherical Core seconds later.

The Core was maybe ten meters across, totally lined with computerized equipment, screens of all sizes and shapes, and countless patch panels trailing innumerable heavy cables. Several mechanical hatches seemed to offer access to the vacuum outside. The designers hadn't bothered with anything like a floor, or furniture. Sitting in zero gravity isn't useful.

Palmer floated in midair, arms and legs drifting limp around him. From the back he didn't look injured, but erratic electricity crackled irregularly along his mesh shirt and pants. The smell of ozone was a lot stronger here, but at least I didn't smell scorched flesh.

Doctor Tansi hung maybe ninety degrees up the wall. His red-and-blue slacks and shirt showed off a lean, flexible strength. His face was locked in a rictus, like he'd been electrocuted. Sweat covered his face, and his chest shuddered from spasms of hard-fought breath. One hand clutched a handhold ring. The other made twitching, trembling gestures in the air, like he struggled with invisible controls.

Tansi's mad gaze flickered past Watford and I.

Then jerked back, and snagged on us.

"Redding!" Watford shouted. "Get Tansi!" He leaped straight across the Core, towards the far wall.

I dragged in a breath and threw myself at shivering, straining Tansi.

I practiced hand-to-hand fighting every day, but always in gravity. After years of training I felt barely adequate when my feet were on the ground. The four-hour Introduction to Zero Gravity Empty Hand Combat course had only convinced me I knew nothing.

Hopefully I knew enough to occupy Tansi for a few moments.

Tansi's gaze met mine. His black, sweat-rimmed eyes held a void as echoless as the empty universe outside Wemm Station.

Soaring towards him in free fall, I kept my hands outstretched in front of me, open but fingers hugging each other. I didn't need to break a thumb.

Tansi recoiled at my approach. His lips twitched around his jammed-open mouth.

I reached for his outstretched arm.

Tansi yanked the limb away.

Inertia kept me gliding towards him. My fingers caught his shoulder, tangling in the fragile linen of his shirt.

Tansi shrieked again. He released the handhold and swung at my head.

Then we were spinning around each other, struggling in zero gravity.

My combat training was all based on the idea of a rationally irrational partner. Someone swings at you, they want to knock your head off. Tansi didn't. He used his arms like clubs, not caring if he struck me with his hand or his bicep. He didn't even make fists.

He'd forgotten how to use his own body.

Tansi twitched continuously in horrific rictus, but he didn't try to thrash around or throw me off.

Jaw clamped open, he didn't try to bite me.

But the spherical room swung dizzily around us, a kaleidoscope of lights and screens and instruments. The more tightly I held Tansi, the more quickly we spun. My head whirled with the motion. If I didn't end this soon, I'd be too dizzy to hang on.

I sucked air against the growing nausea in my gut, wrapped my legs around Tansi's midriff, and locked my heels together behind his spine. That freed up my hands to try to cope with the spasms of his flailing arms.

"Doctor Tansi!" I shouted.

Tansi screeched again. His mouth never moved—the high-pitched monotone howl seemed to rise straight from his lungs. Spittle caught my face.

"It's okay! Nobody wants to hurt you!"

I managed to grab one wrist, then rode the swing of his arm to get my other arm behind his elbow. A quick twist, grab my own wrist, and suddenly I had Tansi in a shoulder lock, anchored by my legs clamped around him.

Most people try to move against that kind of lock, scream with pain, and stop struggling.

Tansi just thrashed mindlessly, lacking even the reflex to pull away.

I pulled the lock even tighter. "Doctor Tansi! Stop this!"

Tansi screeched only centimeters from my ear, driving metaphorical nails into my skull.

My pulse pounded in my throat. Sweat slicked my face, my arms, my back, shaking off into the air as we struggled or soaking into my uniform. I tasted hot copper and bitter adrenaline and a hint of bile.

Tansi convulsed.

Through my interlocked arms, I felt Tansi's shoulder shift unnaturally.

Sudden fear weighted my stomach. My imagination flashed up an image of his skin splitting, some alien shape-changing horror bulging from Tansi's body, a nightmare straight from the stuff my parents wouldn't let me watch.

I gritted my teeth, refusing to release the grab.

Tansi *heaved*—

—and ripped his shoulder out of joint.

His arm suddenly rolled impossibly far back, pulled by the pressure of my interlocked arms.

Tansi didn't cry out, or scream. His convulsions didn't change their rhythm.

Horrified, I released the grab. I'd practiced that lock thousands of times, always with the instructor's warnings echoing in my brain. *This is dangerous. Don't hurt your partner.* I'd learned to release the lock the second my partner submitted.

And here Tansi had destroyed his own shoulder rather than stop fighting.

Vomit surged in my throat.

I caught myself before my ankles reflexively detached, though, keeping myself anchored to Tansi's trembling form.

Tansi kept flailing the arm attached to his wrecked shoulder, somehow not understanding that he'd broken himself. I had to hug his side and duck my head to his flank to protect myself from his wild swings.

We whirled in empty air for a long heartbeat.

I couldn't hit Tansi. A good hard hook punch doesn't do much in free fall.

If I locked another joint, he'd break his own limbs to escape.

Hugging Tansi's flank, I tugged myself around his body to put my belly against his spine, fighting to maintain my grip despite his constant convulsive shuddering. Tansi's arms, even the wounded one, battered my shins and interlocked ankles.

I wove one arm around Tansi's taut, trembling neck, squeezing my forearm beneath his gaping jaw, grabbed my own bicep, then anchored the other hand on the back of his head against his tight, curly hair.

And squeezed.

Not the throat—the throat crushes too easily. But the bones of my arm lay across his carotid arteries.

In seconds, Tansi's struggles slowed.

I fought to slow my own panting.

Then Tansi sagged, limp.

I immediately released Tansi's neck, but kept my legs anchored around his midriff. My lungs heaved as I sucked air and ozone and hints of Tansi's lime cologne mingled with our sweat.

My awareness slowly expanded. Palmer stirred, one hand on a ring in the wall and the other at his head. He breathed slowly and deeply, not like a tired person, more like a guy trying to hold his temper. Watford glared at me from his perch near a medium-duty laser, haloed by disconnected cables.

Too short on air to say anything, I nodded at Watford. I put one hand on Tansi's collar as an anchor and eased the death-grip in my ankles.

Watford scowled. "Scene secure!" he shouted.

Mvouba's head popped into the room—he must have already been on his way up the access tube. "What have you done!"

Watford growled, "We've secured the scene. As you demanded."

"With a field disruptor!" Mvouba pushed off the wall, aiming towards a spot near Watford.

"That was the available equipment, yes."

I glanced at Palmer.

Palmer gave a sheepish shrug. The side of his mouth twitched upwards.

"You may have corrupted every experiment!"

More Congolese crew followed up the access tube as Watford and Mvouba's argument escalated. I happily relinquished my hold on Tansi to two medics and claimed a spot next to Palmer, working to catch my breath.

"Unacceptable!" Mvouba finally shouted. "I'll be reporting on you to my superiors!"

"Go ahead," Watford shouted. "I can use another commendation. My duty—my *only* duty—is securing the Portal. Aliens attack Ring One, you call me. You call us again for some bogus internal sewage like this, I'll bring a bigger hammer."

Choked rage made Mvouba tremble. "We are finished with you, Mister Watford."

Watford smiled. His voice dropped to normal. "But as long as you use a Portal, Commandant, Montague's not finished with you." Watford looked up. "Palmer. Redding. With me."

5

You can't stalk in zero gravity, but Watford sure tried. I did my best to keep up. Palmer grabbed his folded-up khakis from the base of the access tube, tucking them under an arm to scurry after us. I eyed Palmer in the elevator, but he quickly shook his head and glanced at Watford's back.

You *can* stalk in Ring Three's point-eight gravity, the same level as the Portal. Watford marched us to his office. His first words since leaving the Core were, "Take a seat, both of you."

Watford's spacious office looked like it was furnished in Minimalist Neo-Industrial. Bare aluminum walls, with a screen painted on one. Watford's desk looked too small for the room. A little larger than the usual Montague issue, it held only a keyboard and a display. Voice control is nice, but without an implant nothing replaces a keyboard for high-speed information processing. The air humming through the vents hinted at electricity and lubricant.

I eased myself onto a vinyl-covered aluminum-frame chair and leaned back with a grateful sigh. The fight with Doctor Tansi had adrenalized me, but burning that off left me exhausted. My back ached, my arms and legs felt battered and unwilling to move. My lungs ached. With enough gravity to sit but not enough to weigh me down, the chair's thin padding made me groan with relief.

"Problem, Redding?" Watford asked.

"Uh," I started. "No, sir."

Watford reached down into his desk, pulled out a bottle of water, and tossed it at me. "Always drink after a fight," he said. "You should know that."

I fumbled the catch, but snagged the plastic water bottle before it fell.

"Ask for what you need," Watford said. "You *will* get it, but I'm not going to read your mind."

The flat, metallic water tasted delicious. "Yes, sir."

Watford's brown eyes flicked to Palmer. "You said you could handle the laser. I got up there and found you floating half-dead. What's the problem?"

"Normally yes," Palmer said levelly. He sat with one ankle over the other knee, completely relaxed despite wearing only skimpy briefs and a form-fitting fishing net. "But the few systems I have activated are capped at half load."

"You pulled the specs on their lasers," Watford said.

"Tansi increased the power somehow," Palmer said.

Watford's eyebrows narrowed. "Those are supposed to be sealed units."

Palmer shrugged, the lean muscles of his chest shifting beneath the mesh shirt. "The laser was firing at almost nineteen percent over spec. Sir. Given a few hours, he could have punched through the Ring Six wall."

Watford chewed his lip. "Get yourself checked out. I want to be sure you're running at spec. If we need to increase your power reserves or lift your cap, I want it done today. Dismissed."

"Yes, sir."

"But put your uniform on first," Watford called at Palmer's retreating buttocks.

The door slid shut behind Palmer. Watford pivoted his attention entirely to me. "Welcome to Wemm Station, Redding."

I screwed the cap back on the half-empty water bottle. "Thank you, sir."

"Normally I'd have given you a slow morning to adjust to the time change."

I blinked. "Time change?"

"You haven't had a chance to notice, have you? We're on Congolese time here, not Uruguay."

I couldn't help a faint smile. "I was on vacation in the Congo, not three hours ago."

"Good for you." Watford leaned forward. "Let me tell you, Redding. Our concern here is with the Portal. Specifically, what goes into the Portal." He raised a loosely coiled hand, shaking it for emphasis. "The Congolese are the world's newest superpower, and every one of their staffers, from the researchers to the janitors, have something to prove. They started Wemm Station after their Titan colony imploded, and they've got a chip on their shoulder for it." He raised a single finger. "And the bastards at Headquarters who negotiated the contract didn't take that attitude into account."

"So, they want us to handle their crew?" I said.

"One of their people goes space-happy? That's not my problem. It doesn't threaten Earth." Watford leaned back in his chair. "But every time they have a kerfuffle, they call us. We have twenty-four people. Exactly enough staff to secure the Portal and care for our own people."

I grimaced. "How often do they have trouble?"

Watford's eyes narrowed slightly.

"Sir," I added.

He gave a tiny, unconscious nod of his massive head. "The damn fools brought families. They brought their *kids*. Said it's part of their 'cultural heritage.' It's like they're building a colony or something. You get people starting fires for a barbeque. Teenagers mucking with their datacore."

"We have our own datacore?" I said.

"Didn't they brief you?" Watford said.

"I accepted the assignment a couple hours ago. Spent most of that getting here." The back of my mouth still ached, so I took another sip of water. "And helping with Tansi. Sir."

"Not your fault. Fine." An air handler kicked on, and Watford raised his voice slightly. "Montague controls Ring Three. We have our own datacore, our own medical, our own barracks. No HR, one administrator for paperwork. We have a little space on each of the other rings. Our datacore talks to theirs, but it's heavily filtered. You can make calls and appointments and simple queries. And you'll be doing a lot of that."

Appointments? An alien universe, and I'll have *appointments?*

"You get the dirty end of the stick, Redding." Elbows on the laminated desktop, Watford steepled his fingers. "You're going to be the point of contact for the Congolese. And I handled today the way I did specifically for your benefit."

"Sir?" The vinyl chair had started to absorb and reflect my body heat, making my sweat-soaked shirt even more sticky.

"I can't stop Mvouba's people from demanding my involvement. But I showed them that calling me in has *consequences.*" Watford gave a humorless smile. "I instructed Palmer to use the field disruptor against Tansi's laser so that the Congolese scientists would *have* to check every piece of equipment. Every bit of data. It's probably fine—the research has legitimate value, we didn't try to wipe it. So I'm the bad cop. You get to be the good one."

My heart sank. "I'm a babysitter."

"It's not exciting, but someone has to keep Mvouba's people off my back. If they have a problem and want Montague involvement, you get to go along. If they demand my presence, go ahead and ask—but now they know I will scorch the earth."

I made myself take a deep breath. This sounded more and more unpleasant.

"You'll probably work with Lieutenant Habre," Watford continued. "She's Mvouba's security lead. It's her first time in charge of a major facility. If you have a real problem, you call me. Your dossier says you're an adequate security officer. You've been to a few universes. You have common sense, you know when things are going wrong."

Like fun I'm just *adequate.* "I'd like to think so, sir."

"You're a Third, but you'll report directly to me, either in person or in writing. Daily. If something seems off, though—if there's a real problem, something that might get through the Portal back to Earth—you let me know *immediately.*"

"Yes, sir."

Watford folded his fingers together. "Montague is a sharing environment. We normally have few secrets in-universe. This assignment is different. If the Congolese want information from us, they need to file the request through the datacore. You provide them no new information. Portal scheduling, the lunch menu… all of this is confidential. As far as they know, Palmer is an ordinary research cyborg. You are to keep it that way."

Palmer wasn't ordinary? "Sir."

"And our barracks are full. Your quarters are down in Ring Two, with the Congolese, at normal Earth gravity. I don't want you fraternizing with them, though—you eat up here, you shower up here, you access any facilities you need up here. Treat it as a security issue. It's not that I think Mvouba would slip something in your food, but we're responsible for protecting Earth. Medical scan every day, same reason. Besides, some parts of the station, like the core and Ring One, the engineering area, don't have the magnetic cosmic ray shields. If you take a hit of radiation, I want you straightened out right away. Get to know the Congolese crew and their parts of the station, but don't go making friends. And blame me for everything—remember, you're the face of reason. A friendly teddy bear, patiently explaining the rules. With a smile. Any questions?"

I sucked at the inside of my cheek, thinking. "I do, but it's probably best if I start by reading the dossier. Sounds like you want me to get them out of your day."

"Exactly." Watford leaned forward. "Like I said, it's a lousy job. You get two months at it because I don't want anyone bonding with the Congolese. This is not a partnership, it's political garbage. They wanted to build a station, they paid to build the station, they get to run the station. The only reason Montague agreed was because this universe is mathematically identical to our own. It's sheer physics research in an empty universe, no immediate commercial applications, no exploitable resources. You're Montague's eyes and ears while they do it. And if you can help them take care of their little problems, better still."

"Sir."

The thought of the space station had excited me, but now the assignment sounded like I was going to be a rawhide bone tugged between the mastiffs of Montague and Mvouba. If either won, they'd gnaw me to bits. I made myself take a deep breath. "I'll handle it, sir."

"Of course you will." Watford waved a hand. "Take a break. Get a shower, clean uniform. Find your quarters, study your dossier. Dinner's at six, so meet the rest of the team—we don't have an HR group here, but Palmer will show you around. Dismissed."

I stood up. The sweat from the fight had cooled, leaving my uniform clammy. A shower sounded great. "I'm on it. Sir."

I had one foot out the sliding door when Watford said "Oh, and Redding?"

I stopped and looked back over my shoulder.

"Your zero-gee hand-to-hand is *pathetic*," Watford said. "Completely embarrassing. Join the zero-gee hand-to-hand group tomorrow. Room eighty-four, Ring Six. Every night, eight PM, until I say otherwise."

Guiding me to my quarters, my datalink steered me to the elevator and down to Ring Two. When the elevator doors parted to a stunning barrage of noise and color, I immediately realized that the Congolese did things very differently.

Montague furnishes their facilities in a drab, utilitarian style. A photo or a painting on Watford's office wall would have surprised me. The closest the company gets to decoration is the company logo stamped on mass-produced items like metal stair treads and the bottom of white ceramic dinner plates. Montague builds industrial facilities and barracks, not homes. They're factories that might need to be abandoned with very little warning.

The main corridor of Ring Two looked like a broad covered avenue. The ceiling was painted a pale blue indistinguishable from the Congolese sky I'd seen only hours before in Lubumbashi, reflecting indirect light over the brightly patterned wall hangings, woven from cotton or wool or some broad plant-based stuff I didn't recognize. The Congolese famously insisted that hand-crafted materials were inherently superior to machine work, and each wall hanging and painting and rug had a tiny touch of imperfection that indicated a human hand.

The walls had to be metal. But I couldn't see any.

Warmth radiated from the azure ceiling. It wasn't quite as warm as the resort, but they'd certainly turned the thermostat up a few degrees.

We were in a space station, spinning at who knew how many revolutions per minute through an empty void. The air had to be mechanically processed and recycled, filtered to molecular-level purity. But the hall was full of cardamom, ginger, and mint from a communal kitchen nestled a few meters to my left, with tables spilling out into the corridor like a street market. A leg of goat turned slowly over an electric grill, sending its sizzle straight into my nose.

Don't get me wrong—Montague feeds us well. It's balanced, nutritionally complete, healthy, and as tasty as the universe's natural laws permit. The bosses eat the same food we do. But eating in the company cafeteria, it takes real commitment and effort to lose your figure.

Nothing the company had ever fed me smelled as good as that roast goat haunch.

And the people! Montague attracts people from all over the world, each with traditions and garb to set it apart. We sign on to Montague's sheltering embrace and get issued company-issued khaki uniforms. The only part of my outfit that looks good is the leather boots, and I only get those because I'm in

Security. You learn to ignore the outfit and concentrate on the person wearing them.

Here, a Congolese woman in a complexly patterned red and blue blouse and long white skirt shouldered past me without interrupting her conversation with the woman next to her. She spoke liquid French, far too quickly for me to follow. Three dark-skinned men walked the other way, in traditional Congolese variegated green camouflage kilts and darker but similarly patterned tight wickaway shirts that showed off some impressive muscle definition, everyone talking simultaneously yet somehow listening to each other.

Everyone looked athletic and healthy. At the resort, the porter had insisted on carrying my bag rather than using a trolley. Waiters hefted trays of food by hand rather than using a hovertray. Their culture's emphasis on creating by hand applied even to washing dirty dishes.

They'd brought that same aesthetic into an empty universe.

I'd grown accustomed to working with people from all over the Earth. I'd grown comfortable, even relaxed, with the English language Montague used. But now I wore a dull uniform amidst colorful swirling skirts and kilts. The only Latina in a flurry of Africans. The only one not speaking French.

And I'd feed my dirty dishes to a reliable, *sanitary* washing machine, thank you very much.

A couple of children, maybe five years old, dashed past me. One girl ducked behind my legs to peer at the other. "Je te vois! Je te vois!" The little girl laughed, then scampered away behind her friend.

This wasn't an alien universe—this was an alley off some idealized Congolese market square, straight out of a 23rd-century Fabrice Bakila novel.

The resort still fresh in my brain, déjà vu overwhelmed me for a breath.

The short man working the communal kitchen saw me and smiled. "Bonsoir, mademoiselle! Une collation, peut-être?"

I should have brought the phrase book. *Collation*—snack? I'd picked up scraps of lame tourist French during my truncated vacation. "Bonsoir, m'sieu." He flinched at my accent, but when I said "Merci, no, merci," he smiled and raised an open hand.

Nodding to the vendor, I turned and pushed my way deeper into the riot of color, sound, and smell.

The good news was, in two months I ought to pick up some pretty decent French.

Unless that was fraternizing.

I didn't *know* I was trapped between Watford and Mvouba. It might not be that bad. Perhaps my mere presence would dissolve the acrimony between them and soothe their hurt feelings, through the magical power of positive thinking.

My datalink guided me through fifty meters of broad hallway. Each sliding door had a hand-painted label, either with a family name or a type of office. A red cross flagged a medical station. People had set up friendly little stalls, fencing off spaces on the sides of the corridor with brightly-colored wool cloth draped over wooden frames or simple hemp ropes strung between wooden posts. They offered to mend clothing or polish shoes or, like one old lady, read your fortune from your DNA print. You couldn't walk straight down the corridor, but had to weave a little.

No wonder they had security problems. Patrolling this place would be a complete nightmare.

The hall abruptly opened up into another communal area with plush padded seats and intimate wooden tables arranged in cozy clusters beneath vine-cloaked awnings. Along one side wall I glimpsed a half dozen pool tables behind a knee-high red brick wall topped with some kind of blue and yellow flowers. On the other side, a gaggle of gawky school kids tended a row of tomato plants growing from a long low wooden planter. A few people at scattered tables worked with tablets or laptops, or murmured quietly to subvocal implants. I guessed that after hours, this place would be full of relaxing workers.

This wasn't a space station. The Congolese had picked up a whole town, a full-on *city*, and dragged it through the Portal.

Through the plaza and down the hall, I found a sliding door with the Montague logo. It looked just like the real thing, except for the slight flourish at the end of the M that told me that someone had painted this by hand.

Well, they wanted to make me feel welcome.

Or they wanted me to know that they could do better by hand.

I had no idea which. It could have been either, both, or something I'd never figure out if I tried until this universe caught up to ours. I liked to think I had the soul of an artist deep inside. Possibly too deep. I felt reasonably secure in estimating my artistic abilities somewhere below the average rock.

My room was the most luxurious I'd ever been posted in. With thick carpeting, cheerful abstract wall hangings, and a recliner lush enough to make my dad's big comfy chair feel like a bed of nails, it looked like it had been decorated by my step-aunt the Mad Crafter. The air smelled faintly of… fresh-baked cookies? Pie? No, but something baked—vanilla, that was it. A small, irregular, hand-blown glass jar of essential oils sat on the bedside table, reeds splayed from the narrow neck.

What kind of mind thinks *You know what this space station needs? Vanilla!*

I kicked off my boots, settled on the plushly quilted queen bed, and dove into the dossier. I had a little over an hour until dinner, and I needed to devour and digest all this information before something else went wrong and Mvouba called on me to help. I might not have always done as well as I hoped on assignments, but nobody could accuse me of not preparing.

Four minutes later, I had just sunk my brain into the Congolese organizational chart when someone rapped on my door.

¬

I didn't recognize the sound at first—who knocks on a metal door? Normally your datalink asks their datalink to announce you. And the luxurious room had everything else, it surely had speakers.

Annoyed, I looked up from the dossier scrolling across the datalink.

The raps came again—three hollow knocks of knuckles on aluminum.

Back at the resort, the Congolese staff had always knocked. Those doors had been lightweight wood, though. Hinged, not proper automatics.

Grumbling, I swung my feet off the bed and wrenched my sweaty leather boots back onto my aching feet. "Open."

The door remained shut.

I touched my datalink. "Open the door."

"The door is not automatic from this side. The button is to the right of the door."

Who builds a space station with manual doors?

Someone who thinks it should smell of vanilla, obviously. I took three steps across the thick shag rug and touched a red button. The door slid silently open.

The woman on the other side wore loose slacks and a blouse, both in a deep blue that reminded me of the South Pacific, or a toddler's holiday dress, or the intensity of the blueberries imported into the first universe I'd visited. The blouse had colorful shoulder epaulets and a trefoil of rank on the shoulder. Her tightly-curled hair was cut too short to grab but long enough to offer a little protection, her skin like cocoa. She carried her weight on the balls of her moccasins, like a dancer or a martial artist, but had her hands clasped behind her back and wore an expression of ineffable good cheer.

I blinked. "Uh, hello?"

"Miss Aidan Redding?" Congolese accent, of course. She looked familiar— had she been behind Palmer earlier?

"That's me. And you are?"

She stuck out a slender hand. "Belvie Habre. I thought I should introduce myself."

Her warm hand had callouses. "Pleased to meet you." Watford had mentioned a Lieutenant Habre. "You'd be the head of security here?"

Habre's white teeth were surprisingly brilliant. I had to tilt my head back to look her in the eye. "My reputation precedes me. I hope it's a good one."

"Watford mentioned your name." I glanced back in the room. "I was just reading my dossier, trying to get up to speed on Wemm Station. There's a lot to learn, and I'm afraid that I've just been assigned."

"Not to worry," Habre said. "The Montague headquarters agreed to assign a dedicated liaison officer only this morning. When our Exploration Command realized that you were visiting our Federation, they contacted the airline and eased your way. Did you enjoy first class?"

The Congolese had arranged that upgrade? "Er, yes. Yes, I did." I glanced back into my room. "I'm not really set up to receive visitors, but you're welcome to that chair. It looks pretty cozy."

"If I know Montague," Habre said, "they sent you a big thick book of facts to memorize. Full of numbers and measurements and not a single human thing among them. I thought you might appreciate some context first. Could I offer you the Wemm Station tour?"

I couldn't help a little smile. "I'd love to, but I've got less than an hour until I have to go to work."

Habre answered my smile with a grin. "Then we'll have to make it only the best part of Ring Two." She stepped back from the door and held a hand aside.

So far, I liked Lieutenant Habre a whole lot more than Security First Watford.

Too bad I reported to Watford.

I glanced around the colorful corridor, its bustling crowds, the booths of hawkers. A smiling guitarist perched on a stool a few meters from my door, fingers dancing on steel strings, hat between his feet. A boy, maybe seven years old, watched the guitarist, entranced, fists twisting the hem of his kilt back and forth.

Habre steered me away from the path I'd followed to my quarters. "Is there anything you particularly want to see, Miss Redding?"

"I don't know enough to ask," I said. "Surprise me."

"By all means."

Our exchange attracted the kid's attention. He stared at me with big eyes, like he'd never seen a Latina, then dashed off ahead of us.

"I'm surprised you use money here," I said as Habre dropped a small coin in the guitarist's hat.

"What else would we use?" Habre said cheerfully.

"I mean, this is a closed environment," I said. "You know what everyone needs."

"But not what everyone wants," Habre said. "If someone's willing to spend a few Congbucks on having their palm read, why not? Hello, Charity." She nodded at a young woman deftly passing a wooden shuttle through a small hand loom, beneath a display of splendidly woven shirts dangling from a thin wire strung along the ceiling. The woman responded a crooked half-smile, but didn't look up from her craftwork.

"Friend of yours?" I said.

"My sister-in-law."

"You brought your whole family? This is an alien universe!"

Habre laughed. "It is sayings like that which make the Montague people seem so strange. How can you bear to be so far away from your family, for so long?"

I let my gaze study an intricate oil still life of a disassembled datalink, neatly framed and mounted above an artist's booth. "Not everyone is so tightly tied to their family."

Habre shook her head. "In the Federation, your family would know better. Family is what gives us humanity. If we were to understand the earliest days of the universe, but lose ourselves, our whole expedition would be a failure. Ah, here we go!"

The hallway had opened up into another plaza. While the room looked about the same size as the first plaza I'd walked through, the décor was totally different. The tables were a little larger, suited for four or six or eight people. A slender man with graying hair and sagging skin stood behind a wooden counter, slicing shawarma from a jerkily rotating spear of packed chicken while a customer waited. Again, the smell seized my nose and made my stomach grumble.

"Manny has the best kebab on the station," Habre said. "Perhaps you'd be willing to join me for dinner one night?"

I winced. "I'd love to, Lieutenant, but my orders don't permit me. I'm to take all my meals with the Montague crew."

Habre's face clouded. "Silliness."

The old man handed the skinny customer a flatbread filled with sliced onions and steaming slivers of seasoned chicken. "Believe me," I said, "given my choice, I'd join you right now."

Habre pushed the scowl from her face. "At least *you* have good sense."

I took a deep breath. "Something that smells that good doesn't need much sense. Aren't you afraid the station will catch fire?"

"The wood is all treated," Habre said mildly. "It will ignite a little before the walls melt. Same with the carpeting, the clothing. If a fire starts, the computer will douse it before it can spread."

"I'm surprised you don't have firemen," I said.

Habre's scowl returned. "What do you mean by that?"

"Just that—look, you do everything else by hand."

"The station itself has full automatics," Habre said with a hint of anger. "A full range of fire suppression agents, all managed by the datacore. My team will respond immediately, of course, but we handle the human element."

"Of course," I said. I hadn't wanted to make an enemy out of Habre, but I seem to have touched a sore spot. "Really, I meant no offense. The station's just… very different from anything I imagined. It's like nothing Montague would build. My quarters—if I was sleeping upstairs, it'd be okay. But my room here, it's amazing. That bed felt like a cloud. It's like I'm back at the resort."

Habre seemed to decide to let her anger go. "I'm glad you like it. My husband is an artist. I asked him to create your chamber."

"I've been in a few universes, but none where I've thought a good way to spend a day off was to stay in my room to admire the walls."

"Most of those are my Lincoln's work," Habre said.

"Tell him he's very good."

"You'll have to do that yourself," Habre said. "His ego is already too inflated for me to manage properly."

"Well, if you need him to get a critique instead, let me know. It'd take some work, but I'm sure I could find something."

"He would laugh it off. Say that your taste had been atrophied by that horrific Montague aesthetic. To the right, here, then at the end of the hall."

My misstep hadn't caused any lasting harm—or, rather, Habre had decided to let me pass. She was probably as intent on working well with 'the new liaison' as I was on working with her.

At the end of the narrow hall, Habre stepped aside and held out a hand at the door. "After you, Miss Redding."

I raised my eyebrows, then stepped forward so the door slid open.

The room's darkness made its size indeterminate. The only bright light came from the door behind me. Unlike the hall behind us, the air here tasted cool and metallic, shocking after the tapestry of cooking food and growing plants we'd walked through.

The glorious spray of blues and reds and greens covering the far wall immediately seized my attention. It looked like an exploded egg in neon colors, stark against the surrounding darkness, so thickly textured it seemed to pulse with life.

That far wall wasn't a wall.

It was a window.

I took a step closer. "Wow. What is that? I thought there wasn't anything out there?"

Habre's rich voice filled the darkness. "It's a proto-nebula, the Veldt. In a billion years, it will be stars."

"How can we see it? I thought there wasn't any light out there?"

"The window shifts the spectrum. The Veldt is dense, the weight of all that hydrogen holds it together and makes it interact. It's ages off from fusion, but there's much heat and light."

"Amazing." The image was slowly turning, rotating around its axis. No— Wemm station was moving. I couldn't tell how far away the Veldt was, but if it would be more than one star it had to be millions of kilometers off.

A familiar thrill tickled the back of my neck. Inside Wemm Station's steel walls I might have been in an industrial complex. Even the fight in the Hub could have happened in a terrestrial airplane.

But gazing out at the Veldt, I suddenly felt myself in an alien universe.

"We don't understand our own universe," Habre said. "But here at Wemm Station, we have learned much. The earliest days of our universe are so different from our own, that just being here, now, we learn something every day. Our few months of learning have rewritten textbooks. It might even lead to faster-than-light travel."

Faster than light. Thirty seconds after Einstein announced that the universe had a speed limit, people set out to break it. Even my short life had seen half a dozen announcements that FTL was just around the corner.

Still: *so* tempting.

Habre said "The only blemishes on our expedition are these breakdowns."

I pulled my eyes off the Veldt. Habre's outline was a faint texture in the darkness. "Breakdowns?"

"Doctor Tansi was the fifth Congolese to suffer incurable devastation of his neural network in seven months."

Limned by echoes of red and green and blue in the darkness, Habre's face looked unnaturally solemn.

"The first four all died in seconds, or minutes. Tansi's damage isn't as bad— his body will survive. But most of his brain is misaligned. There's not enough left of his mind to reassemble the person he was. Or even *a* person."

My mouth went dry. Restorative neurosurgery is pretty reliable these days. "How does that happen?"

"We don't know. Watford insists that it's a flaw in the station design. All of the victims regularly worked outside the magnetic shielding, either in the Core or in Ring One. And perhaps it is." Tension made her voice tight. "Perhaps these deaths are a risk of exploring this universe."

"But you don't think so," I said.

"The laws of physics are the same here as at home," Habre said. "Our people have checked the station design, many times. We have supercomputers examining every detail of the magnetic shields. But still, it's a unique environment. A previously unknown cosmic ray or sub-atomic particle? Some side effect of the Portal?"

"The Portal's never done that to anyone," I said.

"Never before," Habre said fiercely. "What if we're somehow changed by the transition? Made vulnerable? My people are dying—it requires investigation."

Everything ached to tell Habre that we needed to check every possibility. I wanted to dive into the Montague datacore and compare the injuries to those experienced on other expeditions. I wanted to check with my teammates and go over everything, trying to find some common element.

But here, I didn't really have any teammates. I'd only met a couple of my fellow Montague employees. And I couldn't take this to Watford—he'd tell me this was exactly what I was supposed to handle.

"I have a lot of studying to do," I said slowly. "A little more won't kill me. Why don't you send me your reports on the previous victims?"

8

We can travel between universes. We mathematically describe, and visit, continua with convenient physical laws to make the impossible practical.

But wherever human beings go, we carry the indescribable anxiety of that first meal in a new assignment, standing with a steaming tray, surveying the crowded cafeteria for an empty space where we might fit.

There was a whole empty table at the back, right up against the dull gray bulkhead. Sitting there would declare either that I didn't need to know anybody, or that I felt too insecure to claim a place at anyone's table.

For the first time since elementary school, I felt really insecure.

Every human organization has cliques, and Montague was no exception. One of the most insular teams on any posting was the Portal guard crew, though. A division of Security, they bore the responsibility of making sure that nothing harmful got back to Earth, and weren't interested in talking to the scientists or administrators or even those of us in the rest of the Security crew. They were rightfully paranoid, and I couldn't blame them.

On Wemm Station, the only Montague people stationed here were the Portal guards… and myself.

A round table for four at the back hosted Watford, Palmer, and a lanky woman I didn't recognize. I wasn't going to claim a seat with the boss, no way.

That left two long tables, each with a few gaps between knots of people amidst the churn of unfamiliar faces. The closest group seemed really intense, heads together as they talked but voices sharp enough to form a percussive undertone to the rumble of conversation. At the other end of that table people ate without speaking—no good. I needed to ease myself into a group that already had some kind of rapport, not try to jolt the heart of a dead conversation.

There! And the familiar face wouldn't hurt.

I held my tray chest-high and carefully made my way between the tables to a gap. "Mind if I sit here?"

A couple of people looked up from their discussion. Across the table, one of them was Percival, the Portal guard who had inspected me on arrival. He'd been warm enough, and was the closest I'd find to a friendly face. "Sure thing, ma'am," Percival drawled. "Pull up a chair, make yourself at home."

"Thanks." I set my tray in the gap and perched on the floor-mounted low-backed aluminum seat.

"This here's Miss Aidan Redding," Percival said. "Just came through the Portal today."

"Welcome aboard," the skinny woman to my right said, fork poised in her hand. "Name's Twill."

"San-Chow," offered the chunky native Aussie to my left.

"Pleased to meet you," I said, tugging my napkin into my lap. After my plush quarters, the metal chair seemed designed to rub against my bones. It wasn't any different than any other Montague cafeteria chair.

I glanced from face to face, trying to anchor each name to a set of features. Yes, Montague uniforms have the owner's name stitched above the left breast pocket, but I always notice when someone looks down at my name.

"So you're the long-sought Congolese Liaison Officer," Twill said, stabbing at a slice of yellow squash.

"That's me," I said.

"Good luck," San-Chow said.

"Thanks." I studied my tray for a moment. On some postings, you're lucky if the universe's natural laws permit you to eat anything. Here, my dinner not only looked and smelled like real food, it was actual food, imported from Earth, and exactly to my preferences. Three ounces of salmon filet, grilled to perfection by the datacore. Green beans and a cup of long-grain wild rice, both steamed to retain the vitamins. A mug of thick spice chai. An orange for dessert, already peeled and sectioned and the nasty stringy bits of rind surgically removed.

I'd eaten meals much like this, many times. Nutritionally balanced, healthy, flavorful. My datalink had monitored today's activity and biological markers and transmitted my precise nutritional requirements to the datacore as I'd walked in the cafeteria door. Despite all my travel and the excitement in the Hub, I hadn't burned that much energy.

But right then, I really wanted fifteen hundred calories of hand-made shawarma rolled up in freshly-baked flatbread, from the stall right down the hall from my quarters.

I straightened my back and pulled my shoulders to attention. If I wanted shawarma, the datalink would get me shawarma. A correct serving. Straight from the food stores, chemically prepared to exactly match my tastes.

Right now, perfection felt annoying.

"What did you do to get assigned here?" Twill said.

The light and flaky salmon almost dissolved on my tongue. I reminded myself that it really was pretty good. "I was on vacation at a resort in the Congo. I think they picked me because I'd had a month off, and I was already on Congolese time."

"Sure you didn't piss off someone in HR?" Twill said.

"Why would you think that?"

"Our Twill," Percival said, "labors under the belief that this is the most annoying assignment in Montague."

Twill jabbed her chopsticks towards Percival. "I spent half an hour today telling this so-called colonel that he couldn't take his six-year-old daughter's macaroni art through the Portal to show his mother."

I grimaced in sympathy. Rank might have privileges, but privilege stops with the universe's natural laws. A very short list of items went back through the Portal without extensive testing. "Let me guess," I said. "They're not too fond of the clothing rules, either."

"We got that settled," San-Chow said as he gnawed a lump of something tucked into his cheek like a hamster. A dark, bald hamster. "Took a lot of yelling, though."

"I wouldn't care to hop the Portal in a kilt myself," Percival said. He had more food on his half-eaten tray than I had in total—and part of it was pasta.

Was that meat sauce?

Stupid metabolism.

"It wouldn't piss me off so much," Twill said, "if they were doing real work here. Sneaking stuff back for scientific research? Stupid, but it makes sense. Hand-made blankets and macaroni art, though? I mean, blankets." Her voice went up a notch and picked up Percival's drawl. "Mabel honey, grab me a blanket, the hydrogen's sleeting tonight."

San-Chow gave a little snort of laughter.

"You've got your job cut out for you, Redding," Percival said.

"Happy to help," I said. "I'm just getting started on the briefing, though." The datacore had added a nice touch of garlic to today's beans.

"How much lead time did you have?" Twill said.

I swallowed. "About two hours. Most of that coming in from the Congo."

"Not the best way to study," Percival said.

"You'll barely get started before they rotate you out," Twill said.

"I got the idea I'm a desperation assignment," I said.

San-chow snorted again. "Desperate to keep Watford from going ballistic."

Percival leaned towards me and lowered his voice. "If the only thing y'all do for the next two months is to keep Mvouba and Habre away from Watford, every person on this team will owe y'all a debt of gratitude."

"And not the 'get you drinks' sort of debt," Twill said. "More like 'you need someone to vanish?'"

San-chow's snort was starting to get on my nerves.

"I've read the summary," I said. "What do I need to know?"

"What's to know?" Percival began winding angel hair around his fork. "The natural laws here are exactly like those in our universe. There's no chance of discovering the next telomere binder or memory lead." He lifted the fork to stab a chunk of sausage. "It's all stuff they could get at home, if they could go back thirteen-some billion years." He stuffed the wad of pasta into his mouth.

"It's not that bad," Twill said. "Some of their observations have come up with whole new fields of math. The fabric of space is bent really weird, and the hydrogen interacts crazily. We might be able to use what they learn to compute new universe transitions."

"We already have zillions of universes." San-Chow probed the mass of gently steaming… what the heck *was* he eating, anyway? Some sort of colorless goulash? Whatever it was, it didn't seem to please him at all.

Maybe my rice wasn't so bad.

"Most of them are useless," Percival said.

"And most of those that aren't will 'bend a man's mind past madness,'" Twill said.

"And return breaking the world." The old movie pitch popped out of my mouth instinctively.

"Great flick," Twill said.

"Please," Percival drawled. "*Unsurvivable*? Cheesy as anything."

I'd grown up watching that movie over and over. At my friend Pavel's house, sure, because my folks sure wouldn't let me see that kind of thing. Childhood is the very definition of cheesy. "It's what people know about the Portal," I said. "Go too far, bend yourself to fit a new universe, and you'll go mad."

"The only madness we'll have here is boredom," Twill said.

"And spanking parents for being proud of their kid's art," San-Chow said, bravely scooping a spoonful of his gruel. "Don't forget that."

A new universe fills me with an incredible sense of wonder.

The next week… pretty much ate that feeling alive. Without salt.

I studied the briefing every spare moment, but Habre appeared randomly with a offers to show me another part of the station. Her hair-trigger sensitivity and my inflexible orders made me feel like I was constantly juggling nitroglycerin.

Watford was another jug of nitro. He demanded details on my every interaction with the Congolese. Mentioning that the grill down the hall from my quarters smelled good triggered a twenty-minute rant on the importance of relying on Montague facilities. When I hinted that Habre wasn't all that bad, he drilled me with blowhard questions on the proper security mindset.

Montague employs an amazing variety of people from all over the world. They're the best, but they all live the Montague way. It's like joining the police, or one of those old armies. The Montague rules weren't designed to cope with people who lived in any other way. Watford lived and died by the rules.

Habre showed me most of the station, though, from the swimming pool in Ring Two to the chicken farm—*chicken farm*, on a space station!—on Ring Five, and at least peered through the door of most of the research and development labs. I was briefly introduced to hordes of harried, overworked researchers. It's not that the Congolese worked their people too hard, but just like the Montague scientists, the researchers couldn't stop delving into the fire hose of data. Give a physicist a whole new way to observe quarks and fermions and hawkings, they'll work themselves to death.

I didn't get into Ring One, where the life-support gear and hydrogen scoop fields live, but that area's at one and a third gravities. Nobody goes there if they can help it. It's full of all the machines that keep the station alive, plus these huge tanks of hydrogen they sieve out of the void to feed the fusion reactors. The only reason to go to Ring One is if something has blown up.

When zero-gee empty hand practice rolled around after dinner each night, I was ready to smack someone. Something. Whatever.

Sadly, Watford didn't join us in actual practice.

Zero-gravity hand-to-hand combat is all about locks and leverage. All our regular martial arts assume that you can push off the ground. Without gravity, punching someone's head sets you both spinning through the air. The only thing you can do is grab each other and squirm around until someone gets better position and can lock a joint against itself. It's like Siberian shiu-chitzu, but without mats on the floor. Or the walls. Whichever is which.

All that fancy stuff they teach you in martial arts, then tell you to skip in a real fight? In zero-gee, that's all you get.

An hour a day of practice, for six days, had made me wish I'd paid more attention to tiny joint locks.

At least getting thrown around by my pinky made a nice break from studying the briefing, and my uncomfortable daily meetings with Watford and Habre. And I'd had enough experience with free fall that my stomach had stopped clenching.

Montague's zero-gee combat practice room was shaped like a chunk of curved sausage and lined with thick plush padding, even inside the cylindrical hatch to the Ring Six corridor. The padding diffused gentle white light across the room, stripping shadows away. Instead of metal rings for handgrips, the practice room used squishy hoops as soft as a newborn's toys. The rings could harden on command for advanced drills, but I wasn't invited to those yet.

I'd spent an hour every evening, for six evenings, getting thrown around like an inflated balloon, wearing a loose shirt and billowing pants made of roughly textured cotton. And the score was a whole bunch to zero, everyone-Redding.

But near the end of my seventh day on Wemm Station, I'd finally maneuvered myself into position to try a technique. Percival had this grip like a hydraulic vise, so I attacked the other end. I locked my legs around Percival's knee and planted my feet into his hip and waist so he couldn't double over, keeping his foot tucked behind my armpit. He thrashed, so I wrapped my arms around his leg and straightened to take the ankle lock. Percival's other leg bounced off my back, the angle not letting him get a good blow.

"That's it, Redding!" Watford shouted from his handhold. He was the only one still in a regular Montague uniform rather than a gi.

We bounced off another struggling pair, sending us spinning in a whole new direction.

Percival yanked his leg, trying to break my grip. I clamped down, ignoring the sweat beading on my face and drenching my shirt and my coarsely textured gi. Forty minutes into tonight's practice, our own sweat made every grab slick and thickened the air beyond what the air handlers could purge.

I slid myself out, keeping my feet anchored, and got one arm up over his Achilles tendon. In a flash I had seized my own bicep and brought the other hand up to clamp his toes and pull the foot into place, everything right for the first lock I'd managed since starting—

—and my datalink triggered the practice room's speakers. "Aidan Redding. Security alert from Lieutenant Habre."

I let my breath out in a short, wordless explosion of frustration and released Percival's leg. He tapped my leg to acknowledge end of practice. I unclamped my burning legs and starfished to slow my rotation.

"Redding," Palmer called from his perch near Watford. "Incoming."

I nodded, trying to relax to stop the strained trembling in my back.

Palmer swept me out of the air with uncanny precision. Where I had to jump off something and aim to hit a wall, Palmer adjusted our arc in midair, his cyborg implants somehow imparting momentum. Half a breath later I was grabbing the hand ring next to the circular hatch to Ring Six's main corridor.

Watford had a bladder of water in the crook of his elbow. I grabbed the water with a nod of thanks, then fumbled for hard-wired intercom next to the door. "This is Redding."

Habre spoke quickly, her Congolese accent thicker than usual. "Repairman Daktari Monard appears to have suffered a mental breakdown similar to the others. Can you assist?"

As she spoke I'd sucked water, and had to swallow quickly before I could say, "Where is he?"

"Meet us in the Ring Four airlock. Do you have a pressure suit?"

I'd started to sneak another mouthful of water, but the question set me to coughing. I kept my lips closed to keep from spraying Watford and Palmer, but Watford still glared bullets at me. "He's outside?"

"That is what airlocks are for, Miss Redding."

Palmer whispered, "Sir, maybe I should—"

Watford cut him off with a slash of his hand, which saved me the trouble of smacking Palmer. Calls like this were the entire reason I was here, but punching a cyborg isn't a good idea, even someone as good-natured as Palmer. I'd read the two-page summary on Palmer, just as I'd read every other Montague staffer's summary.

I hoped that we would *never* need Palmer, our final defense against a threat to Earth.

Because if we did, the survivors would all need pressure suits.

Except Palmer, that is. A deep space construction cyborg can withstand almost anything.

"I don't have a personal pressure suit," I said. "But I do have the training. I'm on my way."

"Good." Habre sounded a little less frantic. "We need all the bodies we can get."

"Redding out." The blue light disappeared as my datalink cut the conversation.

"What is your plan?" Watford said.

"Keep them off your back," I said.

"What if you can't?" Watford said.

"If they can't handle it and demand more help," I said, "I'll offer to get Palmer."

"Back at it!" Watford shouted at the room. "You gonna let someone else distract you? Chen, you lost him, start over!"

I guessed that was all the approval I was going to get.

I snagged my datalink from the tiny locker and clipped it to the edge of my gi. Sweaty and in bare feet, I slipped down Ring Six to the dedicated Montague elevator. My datalink used the security alert to have the car in place when I arrived and opened the doors as I approached. Before I could orient my feet to the floor, the elevator began dropping back towards gravity.

I'd had vacuum training. All Montague employees did.

Four whole hours, entering and leaving a sealed vacuum chamber.

How hard could it be, subduing a madman outside a rotating space station where hydrogen atoms screamed past at half the speed of light?

10

Most of Ring Four is Wemm Station's cropland. Because why import lettuce and corn from the rolling green acres of Earth when you can dedicate a huge chunk of your very expensive space station to farming? Not even hydroponic style, but in actual dirt imported from the Congo?

Fortunately, the Montague elevator isn't that far from the Ring Four exterior access, so I didn't have to cut through the cow sheds or anything like that on my way to the airlock.

Airlock.

Outside.

Wemm Station rotated about one point seven times a second. Ring Four was about four hundred meters across. That gave Ring Four a tangential velocity of about 35 meters a second.

If I slipped, I'd fall away from the Ring at almost a hundred thirty kilometers an hour. If I was lucky, I'd hit Ring Three and maybe not skip off it. If I had enough of a sideways kick to miss the next ring, though, I'd be a hundred kilometers away in an hour. They'd come fetch me, and I'd hear about it forever.

Maybe I'd bounce off Ring Four. I could break my neck, or ricochet off into the array of antennas enmeshing the station.

Or pass through the wrong part of the magnetic field, and get the electrical impulses of my nervous system crushed flat.

So: a tragic death, or ignominious fame.

Or hold on tight.

Yes, pressure suits had all kinds of safeguards. We weren't using custom suits cobbled together to cope with an alien universe's unnatural physics. These were right from Earth, and had centuries of experience-backed improvements behind them.

Could those improvements compensate for my whole four hours of experience?

I'd have to hold on really, really tight.

I needed a moment to recognize the scene in front of the airlock. I knew the smells of metal and grease, plus the farm's lush greenery. The faint underlying stench of the pig farm added just a touch of surrealism (although it smells a whole lot better than the chicken farm). The airlock itself was two massive bulky interlocking panels, the same general design that humanity had used for centuries now, set in an undecorated aluminum-walled work bay.

But Montague pressure suits are non-reflective silver, other than your name.

As you might guess, no two Congolese pressure suits were alike.

They were all built to the same general shape, baggy full-body suits of woven metal and tough plastic and cylindrical helmets with broad dark faceplates. Where Montague programs the smart cloth exterior to display vital information, the three fully-suited figures in front of me each resembled African lions, two lionesses and a lion that somehow added the impression of a great thick shaggy mane around the neck's chunky pressure seal.

Habre didn't have her helmet on yet, but the rest of her suit bore irregular leopard spots over rich gold. The spots weren't quite random, instead flowing in currents my conscious brain couldn't quite nail down. Two other members of Habre's security team I'd met briefly held their helmets ready, their suits in a less intricate leopard pattern.

"Lieutenant," I said with just a hint of a pant.

Habre studied me for half a second. My gi wasn't quite sweat-soaked any more—the station's air conditioning had dried most of it out, but I still reeked of hard work. "Are you in condition to go out?"

"I'm fine." I had downed the bladder of water in the elevator. "Bad timing, that's all." I'd met the other two Congolese security officers briefly, and scrabbled for their names. "Bapa. Ramazani. Nice suits."

Ramazani's smile barely cracked the granite of his face. Bapa nodded her chin a millimeter, no sign of the good cheer she'd had during our first meeting.

"Let me grab a suit," I said, slipping into the side room.

The smallest Congolese suit fit me, barely. I really needed the next size down, but the Congolese are all giants next to me. The cloth felt baggy and clumsy, the delicate gloves a little too large, but it would do. My datalink synched to it, triggering the biosensors at my wrists and ankles and neck. As Habre hadn't sealed up yet, I elected to carry my helmet out to the crew, the bulky life-support pack fairly heavy despite the two-thirds gravity.

Everyone but Habre had put their helmets on while I suited up. Habre rolled her eyes as I lumbered out. "Welcome, Montague."

I glanced down.

My datalink had configured the suit's smart cloth as per its programming: dull silver, with the name REDDING spelled out in tall serif letters across my chest.

I felt my face grow red and hot, and had no doubt that behind the other five blank faceplates, other eyes had rolled. "Regulations," I muttered.

Habre shook her head. "Daktari Monard was working on a long wire antenna on the Hub scaffold when he experienced a breakdown." She spoke directly at me—everyone else had already had the briefing.

I wanted to jump in and ask why we were on Ring Four when Monard was overhead, but held my silence. Habre wouldn't have gotten her job without knowing how to lead a briefing.

Habre said, "Monard immediately abandoned his partner and began climbing down Spoke Five." Right by this airlock. "We will intercept Daktari."

Elbow by my side, I raised a hand towards my head.

"Yes, Miss Redding?"

"What about the remotes?" I said. "Can we reduce his suit oxygen just enough to make him take a nap?"

"Monard has disabled the remote," Habre said sharply.

I winced.

"No, it should not be possible," Habre said. "But his suit is not responding to commands." Habre tapped a touchpad on her sleeve. "I'm sending you a security program. Establish physical contact between the palm of your suit and with Monard's life support pack, and you'll force-reflash his life support." Her face was tight. "The suit will immediately stop feeding him oxygen. We'll need to restrain him until he passes out, then we restore oxygen and get him to Medical."

I glanced around at my sudden teammates. "Will it go off if I touch someone else?"

"We're not daft. It's hard-coded to his suit."

I raised my hands in surrender. "I didn't think you were, but I'd rather ask a foolish question than make a terrible mistake."

Habre frowned but said nothing.

My datalink, clipped to the suit's bicep, buzzed. The fifty billion layers of security between the Congolese and Montague datacores flashed up a whole stream of warnings. Bypassing them meant I'd have to take my datalink to the Montague quartermaster for refurbishing. Watford wouldn't tolerate Congolese code executing on a machine integrated into the Montague infrastructure.

I didn't hesitate, but tapped the override button to load the code into my datalink and the suit.

"Do not harm Daktari," Habre said to everyone. "He's retained greater motor function than any victim before him. We might be able to aid him."

I sort of admired Habre's hope, even while thinking that more experience in alien universes would beat it out of her.

My datalink chirped, then Watford's voice bellowed from my datalink. "Redding, what are you doing? I got a request for you to disconnect from the Montague datacore."

Watford had intercepted the request. He couldn't have been watching me in real time—that sort of intercept had to be set up beforehand.

"Sir," I said. "My suit needs Congolese software to solve the current problem."

"Pass it another way," Watford snapped. "The data filters are there for a purpose, Third."

Frustration made me want to scream. Rules have a purpose, yes—but stupid software filters might keep me from saving someone's life. I swallowed bile long enough to say, "Sir."

"Watford out."

The datalink went dark.

Lieutenant Habre's face was a storm ready to break into lightning. "Turn around." Anger harshened her voice.

I rotated.

Habre touched my pack. My datalink beeped a soft warning as she manually transferring the program to my suit. "There. Now give me your helmet."

Why? Habre was already annoyed enough, so I clumsily moved my arm back until I felt her tug the helmet free.

She settled the helmet over my head, sealing the outside world. I felt a sudden huff of pressure all over my body as the suit sealed and puffed an extra few grams of air around me.

I'd gotten myself in and out of pressure suits dozens of times. Most of my vacuum training was putting the suit on and taking it off again. I might not know how to build a space station, but I knew perfectly well how to put the blasted helmet on.

My datalink flashed text above the view plate, rather than right on the screen. SUIT SEALED. CORE FUNCTIONS CONFIRMED. The words ADVANCED FUNCTIONS INACCESSIBLE blinked red. Those advanced functions probably required Congolese software.

"There you go," Habre said, her voice relayed by my datalink into the helmet's speakers. She lumbered around into view. "Good?"

"System reports seal," I said tightly. I'd told her that I'd had vacuum training, and yet, on our first real assignment, she blew that off.

Habre came around to my front and thrust her helmet into my hands. "Good." She bent her knees, bringing her shoulders level with mine.

I stood there for a moment before it hit me.

Putting my suit helmet on for me had nothing to do with my competence. It was about… caring, maybe? Respect? Teamwork? Something like that.

I'd have to think about it when I wasn't about to help catch a mentally broken crewman.

Carefully, I eased Habre's helmet over her short-cropped tightly-ringed hair, giving it the final twist to tell the automatics to start up. "Okay?" I said.

"All green," Habre said. Her anger at Watford wasn't gone, but her voice had grown a little softer. Maybe having me help her with her helmet had reminded Habre that I wasn't Watford.

Then we tromped into the airlock, and out into the hollow cosmos.

11

The airlock opened onto a roomy steel mesh balcony overlooking absolute nothingness. The only people who would see the balcony were construction and maintenance workers, yet the Congolese had built the surrounding waist-high fence and rail out of gently twisted square steel stock, giving the industrial platform a touch of artistic elegance. At every step, my magnetized boots clanged crassly. Two thirds gravity didn't require magnetized boots—but hanging on the outside of Wemm Station did. The half-dozen pressure-suited people around me moved in perfect silence, but the faint vibrations of their steps echoed up from my feet.

At my first step outside the airlock, an automatic safety line of woven steel whipped out of my belt and clamped onto the rail. Slightly reassured, I tromped out onto the balcony.

The bulk of Ring Four loomed over us. Rather than stark spotlights, the Congolese had even arranged their exterior lighting with an artistic sensibility.

The massive white Ring somehow gleamed without glare. A ceramic coating, maybe?

I'd know, if I'd had time to memorize the briefing.

The pressure suit's support system purged carbon dioxide nicely, but it wasn't really designed to suck away the stink of my own sweat from almost an hour of empty-hand combat practice. The way the slightly too large pressure suit hampered my movements made my heart beat a little more quickly—not because of the suit, but because of what the suit represented.

I was in vacuum.

The stillness was a trick of perspective. This part of the station rotated at about thirty-five meters a second.

The safety line had me, but the vacuum still drew my unwilling eye.

I hadn't expected to see stars, not in this vacant universe, but I'd expected a greater impression of space. With no context, the blackness around the Ring might have ended ten meters away or endured forever.

If everything went wrong and I fell away from the station, I'd never even hit a star. Some future alien civilization might find my desiccated remains and carbon-date me at thirteen billion years old.

I'd mess up their physics *forever*.

The thought gave me enough of a chuckle to break the void's hold on my consciousness.

Looking up, the vast gleaming bulk of Ring Four curved away from us, leading to the smaller cylinder of Spoke Five. The centripetal gravity made the spoke appear stationary, rising up towards the slightly smaller bulk of Ring Five, a shining arc in the sky. Ring Five hid Ring Six and the zero-gravity Hub, but the antenna array rising from the Hub's axis of rotation formed a brilliant spire crossing half the sky. With no background to provide perspective, Spoke Five looked like a pillar supporting a glowing white heaven.

But halfway down the spoke, something jerked and twitched and spasmed its way towards us.

Habre spoke from my headphones. "Sahara, Odyn, Aidan, and I will surround the ladder. James. Matisse. Secure the hatch leading down, then back us up."

"Ma'am," I said amidst a chorus of acknowledgements.

We shuffled into place in a tight ring around the descending steel rungs.

Overhead, the twitching figure of Daktari Monard came closer.

He moved… wrong.

Where a normal person would ease their feet down to probe for the next rung, Daktari launched each foot out in a great, swooping curve until it struck the hull of the Spoke, then dragged it up to hook the bottom of the rung before dragging the foot around the rung to the top. His feet and body blocked my view of his arms, but those wild swinging gloves didn't look like any sensible climbing method I'd ever seen.

I didn't see any sign of safety lines, either. His suit should have been constantly launching and retracting safety lines as he descended. Instead, he relied entirely on his handgrips and magnetized boots to anchor him to the station.

Despite his weird motion, Monard seemed to be making good progress.

"Team Warthog," Habre said.

An unfamiliar voice said, "Oui?"

"English, please." Despite the mirrored view plate on the front of her leopard-pattern helmet, I could almost see Habre's eyes flicker at me. "You have Ring Five, Spoke Five blocked?"

"Yes, ma'am," the speaker answered with a Congolese accent thick enough to slice into chunks and fry for lunch. "Daktari won't pass us."

"Good." Habre leaned back to get a better view overhead. "Daktari! This is Belvie Habre. Can you hear me?"

I added Monard's suit to my comms mesh, and instantly heard a husky male voice moaning "Dehors… dehors… dehors…" In a moment he wheezed for air and picked it up again.

I dropped Monard's comms. *Dehors?*

"If he wants out," Ramazani said, "why does he climb down?"

"Nobody else has spoken," Bapa said. "We'll ask him."

I hesitated to speak my idea. I'd know the answers if I'd finished the Exterior Operations portion of the Montague briefing. But at Monard's current pace we had a few minutes before he got to us. "The way he's moving. He doesn't look like he's going to veer off the ladder or anything."

"Yes?" Habre said.

"Once he gets his feet on the deck, he'll be able to move more. If one of us could get a couple yards up next to the ladder, we could hit his backpack and reflash it before he gets his feet on the deck."

"Good idea, Aidan." Habre said. "James?"

"Yes, ma'am." The man in the male lion pressure suit raised his hands in front of his faceplate. The inside of the suit's wrists bulged out, right over where I'd check his pulse, and formed magnetic clamps.

The Congolese had software-reformable suits? Nice. Mine probably was too, except my Montague datalink didn't have the proper software to run it. I could launch safety cables, turn my boots on and off, and adapt my faceplate visuals, but that was about it. If I had a puncture, the suit's fabric would automatically flow to seal it.

James set himself to climbing the Wemm Station wall, held in place by magnets at his knees and wrists. Even at two-thirds gravity, that's hard work. About three meters up, he halted right next to the ladder, just out of range of Monard's kicking feet.

And we waited, watching Monard's flailing descent. I consciously relaxed my muscles one by one, refusing to wear myself out waiting for a struggle.

Three minutes later, Monard's feet came level with James' head. James unclamped his closest hand from the wall, his suit re-absorbing the magnetic clamp. He held his hand raised away from the deck, fingers curled loosely towards Monard.

"Come on, Daktari," James said. "Little closer, that is all…"

Monard lurched and lunged down another rung.

The glove of James' suit rippled, forming a thin tendril of smart fabric data cable that flowed through the vacuum. The cable swung oddly with James' throwing motion, skewed by the station's constant spin, but after one false try James got the end to swing against Monard's bulky backpack and stick.

The cable rippled with inertia.

"Reflashing," James said.

Monard swung another foot down below the next rung, weirdly pulling it upward to probe for his next step.

"Good," Habre breathed. "Surround the ladder, team. We hold him in place until he passes out."

"Right," I said. The semicircle around the base of the ladder tightened infinitesimally.

"Reflash failure!" James shouted. "My suit—"

Before any of us could say anything, James' lion suit rippled.

The smart fabric flowed, squirming over the pressure suit's metallic frame, crawling like a manta ray off the suit and up the data cable towards Monard.

Crystallized air exploded from James, forming a cascade of rainbows.

Smart fabric flowed off James' suit like poured water.

The thin wires of the suit's superstructure were too widely spaced to conceal the sudden rush of blood soaking the man's clothes or the twitching, gaping jaw.

His magnetic clamps gone with the smart fabric, James swung free, plunging back towards us.

I took an involuntary step backwards, hands coming up. My stomach knotted.

Smart fabric suits can't do that. They have fifteen layers of safeguards against vacuum breaches.

But frozen blood spattered the inside of James' suddenly transparent faceplate. The rest of his head and his exposed body, protected from vacuum only by a gaping cage of wire, said I was wrong.

12

I took another step back, defensively raising my own hands in front of my face. The pressure suit's bulk made my every motion clumsy, the magnetic boots clamping me to the steel grid of the balcony, reminding me that we were ants hanging onto the side of a space station in the middle of absolute nothing.

I should have stopped at the Montague armory on my way here. Grabbed a weapon. Fear and dread knifed my guts. Adrenaline made a bright copper taste at the back of my throat.

James had tried to feed software to Monard's suit.

Instead, Monard's suit had ripped the smart cloth right off of James' suit.

A thin data cable connected Monard's suit to James' body.

Habre shouted "James!" and raised her hands to catch his twitching body.

My gaze instantly traced the path between Monard, his suit misshapen and bulging with extra layers of smart cloth, to the data cable, down to poor James' corpse.

And Habre's outstretched hands.

I tried to shout a warning—

—Habre snagged a strand of wire surrounding James' ankle.

Her suit didn't dissolve.

I gasped.

My heartbeat trip-hammered in my ears.

Monard's back sagged, pulling away from the ladder, dragged by James' dangling dead weight and the excess smart cloth now clumsily wadded around his body in ungainly, random lumps.

One hand slipped off a rung.

"Combat mode," snapped an unfamiliar voice, with a chorus of acknowledgements.

I tapped the datalink mounted over my bicep. The words ADVANCED FUNCTIONS UNAVAILABLE flashed above my faceplate.

My blood ran cold.

All around me, pressure suits shivered and twitched. Shoulders, elbows, and knees thickened. The knobby life support backpacks grew armored shells.

My suit might have defenses—but I couldn't activate them.

I'd barely retreated a step when Monard lost his grip and fell sideways.

The station didn't have real gravity. When Monard released the ladder he continued sideways, only seeming to fall because the station was spinning up to meet him. From my perspective he seemed to plunge at a curving sixty-degree sweep, sailing through the air to crash belly-first against the balcony's guard rail right behind another lion-suited security guard.

The cable connecting Monard to James' body yanked tight. Habre jerked back on the corpse, letting her torso move with the force but refusing to lift her magnetized boots from the steel mesh floor.

The bulging Monard folded against the guard rail, then fell backwards onto the balcony.

"Software defenses on," an unfamiliar woman's voice said. "I'm on him."

The lioness-suited person next to Monard studied Monard's upturned-turtle form for a moment, then darted in to slap a hand against a narrow slice of exposed life-support pack.

"Good, Sahara," Habre said.

"Got it!" the lioness—Sahara—said.

Habre somehow got the data cable disconnected from the wire shell of James' suit. "Matisse!" she said. "Take James."

I recognized Ramazani's leopard print as he snagged James' body.

"I'm stuck!" cried the woman.

I whirled back to see the lioness-suited woman kneeling by Monard struggling to wrench herself backwards. Her hand remained planted flat against Monard's life support pack, no matter how the rest of her clawed for distance.

"Sahara!" Bapa shouted.

Sahara's suit burst into brilliantly sparkling frozen air, followed by a ruby haze of flash-frozen blood.

I found myself pressed back against the railing, trembling.

Sahara had put her suit in combat mode. She'd activated the suit's protective software, which should have blocked any malignware.

And Monard had still eaten her suit.

I didn't have even Sahara's ineffective protection.

If I even *touched* Monard, I was dead.

Maybe it was time to call Palmer—*no*. Imagine if that stuff, whatever it was, got into the cyborg's wiring.

Through the haze of wasted oxygen, I saw Sahara thrash within the wire cage of the pressure suit's broken frame.

Bapa and Habre both lunged for her.

My suit automatically dampened Bapa's shriek of "Daktari! Stop this!"

My feet itched to charge in and help. I told myself there wasn't room. I told myself my suit was more vulnerable than theirs.

But a shameful little voice in the back of my head had its own repetitive shriek: *coward*.

I'd faced appalling threats before. I knew I wasn't a coward.

Faced with an attack I couldn't defend against, though, I felt nakedly vulnerable.

"Don't touch him," Ramazani said.

"Right," I muttered.

Monard still lay on his back, now shelled within smart fabric. His arms and legs twitched and kicked, but he didn't seem able to stand. The weight of one suit isn't bad, especially in Ring Four's two-thirds gravity, but the misshapen weight of three suits seemed to have overwhelmed his grotesquely deformed movement.

Habre and Bapa jerked Sahara free by disconnecting the arm of her devastated suit, dragging her twisted figure back towards the airlock. They almost threw her at Ramazani. Her feet barely cleared the airlock before the massive two-part door slid shut. Even in the silence of vacuum, the force of the door clanging together vibrated all the way through the balcony and up into my shoes, making my teeth vibrate.

Habre said "He seems to be stuck. Form an arc, well out of reach."

My suit felt thin. Ephemeral. My tongue wouldn't move from where it was glued to the roof of my mouth.

I made myself step forward, and felt obscurely proud I wasn't the last to fall into place.

"Nobody touch him," Habre said.

I was too scared to make a smart comment. If Monard had control over his suit, he could have it form its own data cables and lash out at us.

"Ideas?" Habre said.

A man's voice said, "We need a computing device that can computationally block attacks from his suit's CPU. Something faster."

"We are *not* connecting Daktari to the datacore," Habre said.

The same nasty little voice that called me a coward now suggested pushing Monard off the balcony. Let whatever had happened to him and his pressure suit spin off into infinite emptiness. Let that hyper-advanced alien race find him thirteen billion years from now.

Instead, I said "Isolation. A solid metal container, a solid metal room. No intelligence in the handlers."

"That'll take forever to make," Bapa said.

"So the machine shop can start work while we figure out a better plan," I said.

Habre jumped in. "I'll send the order."

We'd started with seven people. Now Ramazani was inside, saving the bodies of our two casualties before they were lost to space. I couldn't blame

Habre for the heartfelt decision, but that left us with four figures in a quarter-circle a few meters from the twitching turtle of Monard.

The vacuum looming out beyond Wemm Station didn't feel threatening any more.

But the vacuum right up against me bloomed with menace.

Monard stopped moving.

I had to force myself to continue breathing.

His absurdly overblown suit rippled just as James' and Sahara's had.

A bitter hope flashed through me, that Monard's suit would open to vacuum, solving this problem for us.

Smart fabric flowed off Monard's suit.

No, wait! I thought. I didn't really want Monard to die. He hadn't chosen this—this—no, I didn't know what had happened to him, but surely he hadn't chosen it.

I added Monard's voice to my feed again. His tone hadn't changed. He wasn't even breathing heavy, only repeating endlessly, "Dehors. Dehors. Dehors."

I cut Monard's audio. I wanted to ask Habre what he was saying, but Monard's rippling suit made me hold my tongue. We did not have time to talk.

The smart fabric formed two lumps, one on either side of Monard's prone form, stripping the suit back down to normal size. It still didn't look right, with weird lumps and ripples in the smooth surface.

But he could move.

Monard sat up.

Clumsily, like a damaged robot, he struggled to his feet.

13

Without a word, the four survivors stepped back.

In the middle of our rough curve, Monard stood near the balcony's finely wrought handrail, angled as if one leg had become longer than the other. No—one knee was bent strangely, pointing inward at a right angle to his foot. Had the changing shape of Monard's suit popped the knee within?

Or was Monard himself changing, like his suit?

He looked about my size. Had he always been that small?

Or was he somehow losing mass?

If we restrained him, if we peeled that demonic smart fabric pressure suit off of him, what would we find within?

James and Sahara had already died trying to restrain Monard.

I trembled inside my suit. Bright copper fear burned in the back of my throat, and my stomach clenched so tightly it cast tangled knots throughout my chest and gut.

If I had access to my suit's advanced functions, I would have had the smart cloth repurpose and recalibrate one of the lasers.

Not that I wanted to kill Monard.

Not unless he lunged at me.

But without the suit's advanced functions, I had only a whole suit of vulnerable smart fabric and a couple safety lines. I didn't even have tools—the suit's smart fabric formed hammers and wrenches and whatnot on demand.

My best weapon was the noxious stink of fresh fear-sweat inside my suit.

Monard shifted his stance. His feet left the deck for a heartbeat, the centripetal force only slowly bringing the deck up to meet him.

"Lucy," Habre said. "The latch to the next hatch down. Bend it so it won't open."

"Ma'am." Bapa—I never knew her first name was Lucy—knelt by the hatch, the smart cloth of her pressure suit's glove flowing into powered pliers.

Monard shifted his weirdly bent leg towards the hatch. It didn't want to support him—that knee must be broken, the way he sagged, but the smart cloth stiffened to support him.

Bapa seized the latch in her pliers.

I felt the vibration of twisting metal through the mesh deck.

Monard took another bouncing, skidding step towards the hatch.

One club-like swung wildly at Bapa's helmet, falling short by a couple feet.

I itched to dash forward, to grab Monard, to keep him away from Bapa.

The latch twisted a little more.

"Lucy," Habre said.

"Almost there," Bapa hissed, leaning on her arm, trying to use her mass to torque the pliers more. On Ring Four, nobody weighed enough to tamp down earth around a potted plant, let alone bend metal.

My brain churned. Monard's touch dissolved smart fabric, leaving only dumb wire frames. He didn't have any kind of coordination, just a stumbling shuffle straight out of a brain damage textbook.

Two more steps and he'd club Bapa's—*Lucy's*—helmet.

How many bodies could we drag inside?

I hesitate to call it a plan. It was more of a second millennium anvils-and-dynamite cartoon.

But I wasn't going to let Lucy die, too.

I tapped my datalink. "Disable safety protocols. Manual control."

Text flashed overhead. CONFIRM SAFETY OVERRIDE.

"Disable safety protocols now!" I snapped.

SAFETY PROTOCOLS DISABLED. That text didn't disappear.

"Aidan?" Habre said.

I'd left my comms open—idiot! "I have an idea." No, this wasn't an idea, it was a stunt, it was almost as insane as Monard.

But if it worked, Lucy would live.

Even if it failed, the others would probably live.

The only one who might get killed was me.

14

First, the safety lines. My suit had two, each made of woven and braided steel thread. I retracted one and manually clipped it to the rail directly behind me, then auto-retracted the other.

Monard lurched forward.

Lucy lowered herself further, still trying to wrench the latch permanently closed.

Monard's swinging arm wooshed easily, mindlessly over her head. He wasn't trying to hit her, only shamble towards his goal.

My heart pounded so hard I felt it in my throat, my ears, even my ankles.

"Lucy!" Habre shouted. "Back off!"

"I almost have it," Lucy snapped.

Maybe she did.

But Monard almost had her.

The stumbling madman didn't seem to be aiming for Lucy. He was bound for the hatch, determined to get further down the Spoke towards Ring Three.

The Montague ring.

Where was the Portal? Was it underneath us?

Was Monard maybe bound back for Earth?

No time. Whether Monard wanted Lucy or the Portal, Ring One or Three or whatever, he wasn't getting either.

I reached across myself to swipe a finger over the datalink on my bicep, bringing up the safety line controls. Red crosshairs appeared in the suit's viewplate, wobbling with my finger.

I was *not* shaking that badly.

No matter what the targeting system said.

Monard dropped to his broken knee, making me shudder in sympathy.

No, no time for sympathy either. Bapa was leaning back, but had her arm outstretched, still trying to wrench the hatch's latch so Monard couldn't get further down.

The crosshairs flashed on a possible target. There—*that's* what I wanted.

I locked the targeting system and said, "Safety line launch."

The line lashed out.

My breath stopped.

Even through five meters of line, I felt the spring-loaded hook snap at the end.

Right around one of the rings in Monard's life-support pack.

I still couldn't breathe.

James had touched Monard with a smart fabric data cord, and died. The smart fabric of Sahara's glove had doomed her.

The safety line was dumb. Purely mechanical.

But maybe my suit would start oozing up the line anyway.

I told myself to take another breath, that the air around me wouldn't gush out into empty vacuum.

Monard didn't even notice the impact. He raised his arm to club the hatch.

Lucy snarled and yanked her hand back.

No time to worry.

If I exploded in vacuum, I exploded.

I jerked on the safety line.

The line snapped taut.

I wobbled at the tension—but Monard jerked too.

And I had magnetic boots.

He didn't.

I heaved.

He slid a centimeter towards me.

"That's it," Habre said.

Then she was beside me, her hands gripping the safety line just in front of mine. "We get him up against the rail, tie him up somehow."

"Right," I said.

My lungs ached—I needed to breathe again.

It seemed my suit wasn't going to dissolve, so long as Monard didn't touch me.

We fumbled for a second getting our hands lined up. "Heave," Habre said.

We dragged Monard half a meter from the hatch.

He stopped swinging his arms, staring dumbly at the deck in front of him like the access hatch had vanished.

We shifted our grip up the line.

One of the suited figures stepped towards us.

"Two is enough!" Habre said. "Heave."

Monard fell onto his side and slid, grinding across the deck.

He'd barely stopped grinding when he thrashed his hands to the deck. Before Habre and I could grab the cable again, he'd hoisted himself to his feet.

But he didn't step towards the hatch.

Instead, he lurched in a pivot.

Faced us.

The busted leg lifted, and Monard trudged towards us.

15

Habre instantly stepped back from the safety line. Her helmet swiveled back and forth, and I could almost see her gaze even through the mirrored faceplate.

The safety line attaching Monard to my waist.

The second safety line, anchoring me to the sturdy metal railing surrounding the balcony.

"Let him go, Aidan," Habre said.

"Not yet," I said.

Monard lifted the other foot. Tromped another step. Waved an arm mindlessly before him.

No—not mindless. But not human. Like he didn't know what an arm was for, or how a hand worked.

"If he touches you—" Habre started.

"I know," I said. "I know!"

Instead of disconnecting the safety line, I put my hands on the balcony rail, right next to my anchoring line.

And hoisted myself.

My magnetic boots hung for a moment, then released.

I hoisted myself on my arms, to plant my seat on the thin metal of the balcony rail. My heels kicked against the fence below, the magnetic boots just barely clinging.

"Let him go!" Habre said. "You dying won't help anything."

The rail didn't shift at all under my weight.

"I don't plan to die," I said.

My datalink chirped. Watford shouted in my ear. "Redding! Your datalink's screaming you've left the station, what are you doing?"

"Sir, busy, sir!"

"Whatever you're doing, stop it!" Watford snapped.

I swung a leg over the rail.

"Oh, no," Habre said.

Monard wrenched himself forward. That busted knee skewed wildly under his weight, but he still closed to about two meters from me.

"Oh, yes," I said.

"Redding!" Watford thundered.

"Sir sorry sir!" I said.

In one smooth motion, I swung the other leg over the rail.

All I could see was an endless universe of empty vacuum.

I flung myself into it.

16

I'd skydived as part of my Montague new security employee training.

Not long ago, I'd flung myself out of a falling blimp.

But throwing myself out of a perfectly good space station was a new one, even for me.

How many times can you launch yourself into the void without being called an addict?

This is the last time, I told myself.

For an instant I hung in emptiness, Wemm Station out of sight behind me, feeling like the only solid object in this vacant universe.

Weirdly, my fear evaporated.

For that heartbeat, I felt like in all this universe, there was just me.

Nothing could hurt me.

Nothing could find me.

Peace.

I'd done it so quickly, Watford didn't even have a chance to scream in my ear.

Almost instantly, though, I felt a distant rattle.

My safety line, clattering against the balcony rail.

I slipped away from the station's inexorable centripetal force, for a glorious instant flying free.

But Ring Four spun at a good thirty-five meters a second, and I had about ten meters of safety line.

In a third of a second, inertia snatched me by the belt and whirled me around. The gleaming white expanse of Wemm Station flashed into view and spun away as the station's rotation overwhelmed my puny mass and whip-cracked me into order.

Without the suit's smart cloth and its automatic responses, the shock probably would have broken my neck. As it was, I felt like I'd plummeted from a fourth-floor balcony into a thick inflatable balloon—enough to knock the wind out of me, but not enough to break my spine.

Barely.

Lucy and Habre and the others shouted in surprise, and Wemm Station lurched into view. My vision wobbled wildly, still reeling from the sudden shock of the hard yank on my leash, but I could make out the airlock balcony.

My sudden leap had yanked Monard right up against the low fence. His windmilling arms flailed and his legs thrashed, but the safety line snapped to his backpack held him pinned fast.

The centripetal force made me feel like I hung from my belt, dangling from the cable at my waist, only saved from arching painfully by the automated support offered by the smart fabric suit.

"Everyone okay?" I said.

"Redding!" Watford sounded furious. "Report. Now!"

"I'm anchored to the station," I said quickly. "Safety line. I'm fine. Is Monard secured?"

Habre said, "I believe you have him, Miss Redding."

"I am on my way, Redding," Watford said.

I wanted to tell Watford not to bother, that we had the situation under control. But that wasn't my decision—and besides, I wasn't certain that dangling from the end of a safety line so I could use my mass to anchor Monard in place counted as any reasonable definition of "under control."

Monard's uncoordinated twitching and thrashing rippled down the line, but the pseudo-weight granted by the station's angular momentum and the second safety line kept the motion from knocking me around.

I had picked up a small rotation, maybe two or three revolutions per minute. One moment my feet pointed at the massive bulk of Wemm Station; the next, my head. My sense of balance didn't object, but my eyes insisted that I'd get motion sick, and soon.

Ramazani's voice said, "I have a report, ma'am."

Ramazani had taken Sahara's and James' bodies into the airlock, before they could get knocked into the empty cosmos. What was there to report?

"Go ahead," Habre said.

"They're both in medical pods. No apparent cerebral damage. Doctor Nile is examining them now."

Relief made me go limp in the suit as the rest of Habre's team exploded in cheers. In the explosions of frozen air and ruptured blood vessels, the shock of seeing smart fabric crawl away, I'd forgotten that vacuum didn't instantly kill. If someone's brain survives to reach a medical pod, if a scrap of life remains, we can regrow damaged tissues. I'd needed half my right hand regrown myself, not long ago.

Regrowing a hand itched fiendishly. I didn't want to imagine what regrowing your skin and your eyes would feel like.

If I'd had time to train properly for this mission, the trainer would have reminded me that vacuum was survivable. Montague would have sent me to one of the low-Earth-orbit stations to drill exactly that—and a hundred other emergencies—until I knew it in my bones.

I was seriously unprepared for Wemm Station.

Overhead, Monard twisted against my weight tugging at his shoulders, falling back against the railing.

One of his feet left the mesh floor.

A shiver went up my spine.

"Uh, Habre," I said.

Habre didn't answer. She hadn't even heard amidst the fading cheers.

"Lieutenant!" I snapped. If she acted quickly, if she used one of her own safety lines—

Monard's second foot left the deck.

His overbalanced, deadly form plunged over the railing.

Straight at me.

17

Angular momentum saved me.

When Monard stopped touching Wemm Station, he continued in the same direction he'd been going, perpendicular to the platform's position, while the station itself rotated away. He dragged me after him, then the safety line snapped taut and he swung into place further from me.

Tied halfway between Monard and the balcony railing, I got snapped, thrown, whip-cracked back, then wobbled and spun as the lines slowly steadied out.

Oh, and that slow rotation I had as I dangled there? I'd wrapped the two safety lines around each other. All that came undone in about three seconds, giving me a whole new dimension of nauseous spin.

Once the cable finished thrashing, though, the worst was over. I hung halfway between the airlock balcony and Monard, trying to calm my bitter stomach and hoping that the safety line was as strong as the manual said.

Habre called for a service scooter to come fetch Monard, confining him in a dumb metal crate. I felt nothing but relief disconnecting from him.

Then I retracted my own safety cable so Habre and the others could help me over the rail. They congratulated me all the way into the airlock.

I felt downright triumphant until the inner door opened.

Watford stood about five meters from the airlock, leaving plenty of room for everyone to traipse in. His muscular arms were crossed, the fingers of his exposed hand clenching his massive bicep. His jaw was set hard enough to use as a hammer. And I hadn't seen that much controlled fury on anyone's face since the Montague vacuum suit instructor found one of the new people adding helium to another new recruit's rebreather.

I unlocked my helmet and reached up to remove it, but Ramazani's hands were already there. I stifled my urge to slap his hands away and let him twist the helmet off. The work area's aroma of green crops and distant pigness hit my nose and tongue like a bucketful of life after the pressure suit's filtered purity, but I sucked it down as quickly as I could and said, "Sir—"

"Redding," Watford said, cutting me off as efficiently as a sledgehammer. "You and I will speak about Montague regulations later." He didn't even look at me, but kept his attention on Habre's suit. "Unsuit *immediately*."

The brusque answer left my stomach burning with sudden bile. I bit down a dozen responses. "Sir."

Ramazani had started to crouch so I could help him remove his helmet.

Instead, deflated, I turned away and trudged around the corner into the locker room. The twisting hairpin corridor separating the lockers from the airlock did nothing to block sound.

I knew exactly when Habre's helmet came off. That's when Watford bellowed "Lieutenant Habre. Would you care to explain why the Montague liaison officer jumped off the station just now?"

"The situation was most serious, Mister Watford."

"And why was she in such a dangerous position in this serious situation? She is a *liaison*."

I stripped out of the suit as quickly as I could, setting the helmet on its shelf and tapping buttons to unseal it. I still wore my gi. It had picked up a whole new panoply of stinks: exercise sweat from the zero-gee practice earlier this night, fear sweat from watching smart fabric betray two people, shock sweat, nausea sweat…

It might be simpler to burn the outfit.

A Congolese I didn't know came in right behind me, helmet under his arm. We'd met, but only after he'd put on his helmet. He offered a sad look and a sympathetic shake of the head as Watford and Habre tore into each other.

"You endangered one of my people," Watford snarled.

"Miss Redding acted to help save lives, on her own initiative."

"You should never have placed her in a position that *required* such actions."

If I didn't get out there soon, they'd kill each other.

I sat down to shuck the suit off my feet and made to hang it back in place. The unfamiliar Congolese waved me off, indicating the doorway. Watford and Habre had stopped letting each other complete even a sentence.

The only reason I didn't run full-speed out was that the hairpin privacy corridor didn't offer enough distance to get up to speed.

Watford's arms weren't crossed any more. He had his hands raised, though— not in fists, but flatly, with his fingers held snugly against each other, so that if Habre struck he could counter without breaking a finger or a thumb.

Habre stood tall, her hands deliberately clasped behind her back as if daring Watford to punch first.

Both fell silent when I emerged.

"Sir," I said.

"Redding," Watford growled. His nose wrinkled—apparently I stunk worse than the pig farm. Great. "With me."

"Sir," I said.

"Thank you, Miss Redding," Habre said, her tone hard enough to break rocks.

Watford was already spinning on a heel. "Redding!"

"Sir." I gave Habre a nod of thanks and trotted after Watford.

Watford said nothing as he stormed to the Montague elevator.

I trotted after, suddenly weary to my marrow. I'd done most of an hour of free fall hand-to-hand combat practice, then had more than one moment of adrenaline-fueled fear, inspiration, and terror. I needed a shower and about twelve hours sleep.

Watford's back told me I was out of luck.

The elevator with the octagonal Montague logo was waiting for us. Watford tromped in and swiveled to face the door.

"Sir," I started.

"Wait for my office," he snapped.

I fumed.

What was I supposed to have done? Outside that airlock, touching Monard meant death—okay, not death, but explosive decompression is serious business, and soon we wouldn't have had anyone to drag the victims into the airlock and throw them in a medical pod. We hadn't had time to discuss a plan—as it was, he'd almost gotten Bapa—Lucy.

I hadn't signed on to Montague to be a liaison, I'd signed on to see new universes, advance human knowledge, be at the very fringe of knowledge and exploration. Not to listen to a tin-pot despot rant and rave.

No, I'd accepted this assignment.

Gladly.

Maybe I should have stayed in the Congo resort.

18

I trailed Watford into his sterile office on Ring Three, imagining all sorts of responses for when he started chewing me out.

I wouldn't talk back. I wouldn't yell back.

I'd be calm, and assertive, and declare my refusal to let people die just because I was supposed to be a lowly liaison between the Congolese and him. If he wanted a flunky who would stand by and watch while everything fell apart, he needed a different Security Third.

Watford hadn't even sat down when he said, "Good job, Redding."

The indignation that was keeping me upright gushed out my spine, leaving me dizzy. "Sir?"

Watford tossed me a bottle of water from his small cooler. "I watched everything. You assessed a situation, evaluated the facts at hand, created a plan, and acted, all under pressure."

"Uh…" I fumbled for words. "Thank you, sir?" The water tasted delicious, cutting through my own stink.

"You could have been a little smoother, but that'll come with experience. Screaming in terror is poor practice."

I stopped. Had Watford cracked a joke? "Scream, sir?"

"When Monard came off the balcony and you got thrashed around."

"That wasn't a scream, sir. It was a shout."

Watford's eyebrows arched. "A shout?"

"Like on a roller coaster."

He smirked. "So next time, try a little more glee and a little less I'm-going-to-need-a-clean-uniform."

"Sir." I relaxed a little. "So all that with Habre—"

Watford's flicker of good humor vanished. "Oh, I'm furious with her. Her people should have handled that. If anyone is going to throw Montague staff off this station, it's going to be me." He shook his head. "The Congolese don't understand that this is a different universe."

61

"Isn't it just like ours?" I took the chance of not saying *sir*.

Watford let that pass. "Even if the natural laws haven't changed, it's a completely alien environment. We're right up against the Big Bang here. Anything can happen. Anything did—I've never seen smart cloth behave like that, I'll be sending the video back to Montague for evaluation. See what the historians think of it." He leaned forward. "Before I send you to the showers, is there anything you want to tell me?"

I took a sip of water and a deep breath to buy myself some time. *Habre's not that bad?* No, he'd chew my head off. *You've made my job a lot harder with that argument?* No, he didn't care. Instead, I said "How would you feel—I mean, what are your *thoughts* on me requesting a Congolese datalink?"

"Going native on me?" Watford said.

"No sir. It's just…" I took a deep breath. "I could have used it to operate the Congolese suit. And access the Congolese datacore while maintaining separation with ours. Maybe I can do some research, give them hints, help them figure what's happening."

Watford studied me.

I hauled up a mask of alertness and tried to push the fatigue off my features.

"Redding," he said slowly. "What would have happened if you'd had full control over your suit?"

I blinked, not really understanding the point of the question. "I… I would have had more options."

Watford shook his head and leaned forward on his desk, palms flat against the metal. "I studied your record, Redding. You take action. Given the chance, you *leap* into action. If you see a wreck, you run to help."

"Sir."

"In most cases, I admire that. Montague needs people like that. People who don't have to make a conscious decision to override their natural freeze-or-flight instinct." Watford tightened his lips and kept shaking his head. "But here—if you had a datalink today, you would have charged in to help. You would have fired a data cable to upload the program. If someone beat you to it, you would have grabbed Monard's suit to deliver it the hard way." His gaze drilled into my skull. "Either way, you would be lying in the Congolese medical center right now. *If* you were lucky."

I opened my mouth to argue—but found I couldn't.

Watford was right.

"Set aside that nobody gets my people killed but me," Watford said. "Even ignore the contractual repercussions should a Montague employee get herself killed defending the Congolese. On a purely personal level, you've learned your role quite well. I don't want to take the time to train a replacement. And if something *does* happen to you, I'll put Habre's head on a stick as a warning for her replacement."

"Sir," I said. I'd fought the urge to defend Habre this long, but I couldn't let this pass. "Things do happen, sir."

Watford's face took on a distant, thoughtful look for a breath. "I know that, Redding. I know that. too well." The thought passed. "But they own their station. They own their people. Montague's regulations are designed to protect people. If they want to write their own rules, they have to live with them. Or learn better."

Our way isn't the One True Path. These people just live differently. But I was too tired to argue further, especially with Watford, and let myself slump a little in the chair. "Sir."

"All that said…" Watford leaned back. "I'm certain Habre will issue you a Congolese datalink."

I straightened in surprise.

"But remember, Redding: if you use it to get yourself killed, everything will come apart here until we finish training your replacement." Watford studied me with just a hint of sorrow. "The Congolese are expendable. You—are not."

19

I'm not sure I slept. I don't remember time passing. Maybe I only blinked before the alarm rousted me. I staggered in to the very tail end of Montague's breakfast up in the Spartan mess hall, sore and achy and eyes burning.

The whole crowded room erupted in cheers and applause.

I stopped in the door, shocked awake. Even the smells of eggs, salsa, and coffee couldn't jump-start me that quickly.

"Teach *me* to bungee jump!" a Portal guard I hadn't yet met called.

"That's showing them!" San-Chow shouted, clapping.

I felt excruciatingly aware of the hot flush creeping into my cheeks and up my ears.

As the noise subsided, Percival said, "It was pretty cool," hoisting a coffee mug as if to toast me. "At least until the bit where y'all screamed like a spanked baby."

Laughter sloshed between the metal walls.

The only way out was through. "That," I said, drawing myself up straight, trying to ignore my bonfire blush, "was not a scream, thank you very much. That…" I raised a finger. "Was my ancestral battle shriek."

Fresh laughter and applause erupted.

And Watford, sitting at his little table with Palmer—was that a *wink*?

I took the opportunity to march myself forward to the meal slot.

The duty officer would have watched last night's incident. The video must have flown around all of Ring Three before I even got back to my room. It was probably even going around the Congolese sections. Embarrassment made my face feel aflame.

At least the datacore knew I'd been working—it gave me an extra egg, both *fried*, and two extra slices of bacon.

Apparently the machine figured that hanging over certain death burned calories.

No, it didn't figure. It knew.

The real surprise came when I turned around.

I'd tried to move around each meal, sitting with different groups as much as possible. Everyone had made space for me and talked politely.

Now, four different hands went up from four different parts of the room, waving me over.

All of a sudden, I wasn't the Congolese Liaison Officer, responsible for keeping a bunch of annoying outsiders away from the folks doing the real work of defending the Earth.

Now… I was one of the cool people.

20

Habre thanked me for catching Monard, and tried to apologize for last night's shouting match. When I brushed that away and requested a Congolese datalink and complete access to everything on the victims, she seemed relieved that she could do something for me.

I claimed a temporary office in the Congolese Ring Two: nine square meters with full display walls, a keyboard, and a rolling office chair that looked like it dated back to the Typewriter Age. I plugged in the datalink, and got to work.

Well, I tried to.

Back on Earth, any datalink I used would grab my personal settings from the global network. The Congolese datacore, floating in another universe, didn't have that information. I spent most of an hour trying to get the Montague datacore to send my profile to the Congolese datacore, repeatedly stripping out layers of settings trying to squeeze a useful work environment through the security protocols.

Eventually, I surrendered and started configuring the new datalink by hand.

I was finally ready to work when my Montague datalink pinged me for lunch. I ached to dive into the data instead, but now that I had an opening with my fellow Montague staff I needed to make all the friends I could.

The datacore gave me a second piece of quiche at lunch. Did I need that much protein after last night? Or was the datacore trying to apologize for giving me a headache this morning?

Don't humanize the machines, I reminded myself.

And plunged into the victims.

Or, rather, tried to.

I had preferred data correlation programs, all available in the Montague datacore. The Montague system absolutely refused to accept complicated data from the Wemm Station datacore, though. After battering against that security layer for a while, I arranged for my Congolese datalink to strip the data down to matrices—rows of numbers, separated by commas. The Montague security system snarled, but accepted it.

By bouncing back and forth between the two systems, I eventually managed to assemble a lopsided but usable set of analysis tools and data. I'd also assembled a headache like a hundred-penny nail driven into my right eye and a cramp in my neck.

Once I could do useful work, though, I found…

Nothing.

Six victims. Four died within minutes, their neural flows devastated. Doctor Tansi had survived, but his brain remained scrambled. The medical staff had him floating in a suspension pod, right next to Daktari Monard. They didn't have much hope for stabilizing either.

Three of the victims were Congolese. One came from the Sudanese Sovereign State, one from Zanzibar, the last from the Irish Protectorate.

No common medical details—I don't know medicine other than first aid, but I can compare and contrast information to seek out correlations.

Five parents. All six had family members on Wemm Station.

Two home brewers.

A soccer fiend. Did Wemm Station have a soccer field?

Two people who went outside Wemm Station regularly. One whose work had taken him outside three times in five months. The other three had stayed within the aluminum shell.

A variety of ages, hobbies, and family members.

No signs of substance abuse—Monard had just a touch more whiskey in his diet than advised, but the Congolese datacore hadn't registered any concerns. Maybe Monard's metabolism thrived on booze.

We did have one new information source, though.

Monard's suit.

A Congolese engineer had attached a data cable—not one made of smart fabric, but an actual hard-wired plastic-and-silicon data cable. I'm more familiar with technology than medicine, but even so I had to rely on the engineer's summary. Thanks to the Congolese datalink, I was able to get updates as the engineer doing the examination made notes.

Nothing. The suit's processors were even more disrupted than the human minds.

I took a break for a snack and to massage my head. This was worse than my college senior research paper on the twenty-first century Himalayan global warming trials.

I worked through dinner.

For the first time since arriving, the Montague datalink didn't ping me for zero-gravity unarmed combat practice.

Habre didn't interrupt me.

I finally fell into bed, exhausted and aching both physically and mentally, my brain full of a million irrelevant facts. I hurried through my morning workout, barely paid attention to breakfast, and plunged right into the data.

This wasn't my responsibility. I didn't need to be sitting there in an oversized chair that wouldn't crank down low enough for my feet to hit the floor, staring at a wall display, stuffing information into my head, turning facts around to make them fit like jigsaw puzzle pieces, polishing my headache and exploring data I didn't quite understand.

But this thing, whatever it was, was destroying people. And finding an answer—even a clue—was worth several headaches much worse than the one pounding a syncopated rhythm between my eyeballs.

And just before dinner on the second day, I pulled a recalcitrant pattern out of the noise.

21

I'd grown to loathe my temporary office. The display screen walls, completely covered with graphs, images, frozen video clips, and streams of data I'd shoved to the side, blurred together into a tangle that seemed to knot inside my tired eyes. My stomach grumbled. My mouth tasted like old socks.

And the stupid chair tortured my spine like a medieval rack. Why did the Congolese have to be so blasted tall?

And the data I had was pretty minimal. Barely notes, on something barely above statistical noise.

But it beat the nothing we had.

If I was still in college, I'd write up a formal report, dress it in a nice skirt and a silk blouse, ask a friend to recommend cute shoes for it, and send it to

Professor Watford. Montague researchers made their reports even more fancy, with specific formatting designed to fit into the company's libraries.

I wasn't a researcher, though. The biggest risk to my college diploma hadn't been the tests, or the studying, or the ethical challenges presented in a criminal justice degree.

No, what had almost ruined my college career had been the Global Research Foundation Citation Format.

Instead, I prepared a simple business memo, listing my conclusions up at the top, half a dozen supporting paragraphs, and a bunch of links to data sources at the bottom. The two different datalinks bit me here: a few chunks of information appeared only in one datacore or the other, so I had to make two separate versions, each flagged with "available in other datacore" scattered here and there.

By the time I finished, the headache behind my right eye had spread to my left. My tongue felt parched. My stomach grumbled about skipping a second dinner, demanding I march up to Ring Three and grab a bottle of water and a sandwich before telling anyone anything.

I was hungry enough, the datacore just might give me my own pasta dinner.

But hungry or not, people were losing their minds.

And the deaths, the losses, were happening closer together.

I sent the copy with Montague links to Watford, adding a businesslike note that I was about to send a similar note to Habre. She got a more personal note, saying that I wanted to talk to her about some interesting things I'd found, and attaching the version of the memo with the Wemm Station links.

A Montague employee who got a memo like this, about something destroying people, would have used the datalink to call me right back.

I had a few minutes to rest until Habre knocked on my door.

I climbed out of Death Chair, closed my eyes, and tried to touch my toes. My lower back gave its own ancestral battle shriek. I bent over as long as I could, until the blood rushing to my headache—uh, *head*—made me feel almost too dizzy to stand, then started twisting at the waist and rotating my shoulders.

Habre knocked. "Miss Redding?"

I glanced at the datalink. Four minutes and forty-five seconds—she must have run. At least a little stretching had relieved the worst of my aches. "Coming," I called, reaching for the button.

Habre skipped her usual pleasantries. "You said you found something?"

"Come on in, I'll show you." I hoisted my Congolese datalink. "I thought you'd want the whole presentation."

Habre's face looked ready to burst with tension.

I licked my lips.

Her eyes flicked to my face. "Did you get dinner? Lunch—no, breakfast?"

"Breakfast," I said.

Her gaze bounced up to the countless graphs and images on the wall, then back at me. "I would have my people bring you a meal," she said.

I shook my hand. "I know you would. Let me show you this, then I'm getting a snack, taking a headache pill, and falling into bed. Forget brawling in vacuum. Desk work is what's going to kill me."

Habre's mouth twitched in a brilliant smile, then faded. "Show me."

I set my Montague datalink to record, then picked up the Congolese one. "Your datacore has the very latest scientific information."

"And a complete cultural record," Habre said.

"Of course. But it's the scientific part I need to focus on now. Montague's datacore has much of the new research, but they've curated historical research as well." I didn't add, *and not even a novel or a serial unless one of the staff brings it*. "In some of the universes we visit, the best technology you can get is a forge and anvil, or uranium fission, or, or whatever. We're supposed to study that in our off hours."

Habre frowned. "All right."

"The victims don't seem to have anything in common, so I turned it around. Both Tansi and Monard moved strangely, but kind of similarly. I had the Montague datacore search for people who moved similarly. I thought maybe some kind of cerebral trauma."

"We performed a full medical analysis and comparison," Habre said.

"Your records aren't as complete," I said.

"I assure you, our medical records are—"

"Medical, yes." I took a deep breath. "The Windsor Free State. Right at the end of the Blue Tomato War."

Habre stopped. She closed her mouth. "Yes, that is—something we would not have brought."

"I don't blame you. But when you're out here, you might need *anything*." I aimed the Congolese datalink at the wall. "When they ran short on foot soldiers, the Windsor Czars attempted computer-driven personality reconstruction of political prisoners." I tapped the datalink.

A frozen image swelled to dominate the wall, flickered, and moved. The image was shaky, the camera maybe a meter off the ground, the resolution terrible. According to the historical notes, the photographer had taken the video with a camera hidden in a belt buckle.

I let the video run for a few seconds. Long enough for Habre to see the man's weird, looping footsteps, the windmilling arms, the gaping mouth. For her, I'd left the sound off. I'd also cropped the video. The expression on the victim's face was agonized enough without adding the medical tech. (No, the tech wasn't agonized. He was bored, which was worse.)

When I stopped the video and shrunk the image, Habre's face had gotten a little pale and her lips tight. Her own imagination had filled in what I'd cropped out. The human race might have reached its golden age, but every school kid learns just how much blood we spilled getting here. And nobody likes having that history brought up.

Habre needed a breath to steady herself before saying, "Yes, that looks very similar. Did they—do you know the cause?"

"Interference," I said. "They didn't understand how the brain works, and even if they had, they didn't have the computing power to dismantle and rebuild a personality. Even now, most governments exile irreconcilable deviants rather than attempt to fix serious psychopathy." I wanted to sag into the chair, but it was too high for comfort. "I compared the brain scans of the Windsor victims to our injured people."

"And?" Habre said.

"Not even close. But you have really good analytical software in your datacore, so I played for a while." I swung the datalink to another frozen window, expanding it to run the length of the wall. "And this is what the software generated."

The detailed graph dominating the wall looked something like an old-fashioned seismograph or EKG: one line, wobbling up and down. Unlike those, however, the curves had chaotic, irregular shapes. At some points the line went into pure right angles, oscillating across the axis like an AC power graph.

Habre peered at the wall. "What is this?"

"I used the Windsor techniques for measuring and graphing brains, and extracted everything that wasn't in Tansi's normal mental patterns. And look at this." I swiped the datalink to bring two more graphs up below the first. "This is the same transformation done on victims three and four, their mental patterns."

Habre's lips narrowed in concentration. "Nile and Dancer."

I nodded. "Not the same, but see—the same kind of spikes here and here, the same blocky shapes here and here. I'm not a mathematician, but it looks like a chaotic arrangement of the same components." I took a deep breath. "The first two, their brains were too badly hurt. Not enough to analyze."

Habre nodded. "So that's a commonality between three victims?"

I shook my head. "Four. Monard's got a twist, though."

"You have something more twisted than this?"

"Monard's brain scan doesn't match. But there's interference throughout the logic circuits of his suit."

"The suit has this pattern?"

I shook my head and added a fourth twitchy, squiggly graph to the wall. "This is a combination, extracted from Monard's brain scan and the suit's management module."

"But—" Habre shook her head.

"It's the same interference, split between the two," I said.

Habre raised her hands. "Did you find anything that could impose itself like that? On both a human being and the pressure suit's processor?"

I shook my head. I'd finished my presentation. If Habre didn't say anything, I'd make my recommendations. But if she was competent, she'd take it from here.

Habre drew a deep breath. "I will disseminate this throughout the research teams," she said. "If anybody has seen this, created it, we will know."

"Good," I said. "I included the datacore's work. I'd suggest you have a real mathematician look at it. There might be a better way to analyze the data, an easier way to view it. This is just the… the most obvious way. Copying others' discoveries."

Habre stood straighter. "Thank you, Miss Redding."

I rubbed my forehead. "Happy to help. If it helps. This might be nothing."

"Most leads are," she said cheerfully, shifting a shoulder as if to turn. "But it's the first proper lead we've had."

"One more thing before you run off," I said.

Habre froze halfway through her turn.

I said, "Look at the amplitude."

She peered at the graphs.

"The earlier cases have much more intensity than the newer ones. The effect decreases by about two-thirds for each case. See the Y scale, there and there?"

"That's part of how Tansi and Monard survived," Habre said.

"Tansi had a voice," I said. "Well, he made sounds, at least. And Monard, he kept saying 'dehors' over and over again."

"Outside," Habre said. "He was saying *outside*."

"How much more out could he be?" I tapped my finger on his graph. "But the next time, if it's only a third as serious, it might look like a stroke." Or a headache, I thought, resisting the urge to massage my temples.

"I'll let Medical know as well," Habre said.

"The way they're getting closer together," I said, "the next breakdown could happen any minute."

"Leave it with me," Habre said. "Anything else?"

I shook my head.

"Yes, there is," Habre broke a smile. "Get your meal and your rest, my friend."

"Yes, ma'am," I said with a chuckle and a slapdash salute. I'd have to snip this bit off the recording before sending it to Watford.

The door had barely slid shut before my Montague datalink buzzed.

Watford's booming voice tapped another nail into my headache. "Good work, Redding. If they can't find their problem with that kind of road map, they don't deserve to be out here."

I couldn't help a flinch. He must have watched the recording as I made it.

And I'd saluted Habre—Watford was going to chew me out so hard, I'd have to stand to eat breakfast. "Thank you, sir."

Watford said, "Now grab a sandwich and get up to Ring Six. You missed practice last night. You have *just* enough time to make it, and you owe Percival an ankle lock."

22

Between food, exercise, and helpfully kicking the whole problem over to Habre, I slept like the dead. Breakfast tasted delicious, and while my moment of glory had passed, my Montague co-workers retained their cheer towards me. I was able to put my attention into studying the vacuum operations manual—a little late, yes, and I hoped I wouldn't need it, but still.

To my surprise, just before lunch Habre used my Congolese datalink to ask me to meet her on the other side of Ring Two. Normally, she just appeared and knocked on whatever door I was behind. Rather than hiking a kilometer, I grabbed a tram car and let it whisk me there in a quarter the time.

I found Habre in a common area painted in a thousand shades of green, sitting at a two-person table beneath an awning draped with lush grape vines, picking at a small plate of chicken shawarma. Half a glass of mango juice, thick and rich enough to be called "slurry," sat ignored by the plate.

But she worked up a smile as I approached. "Miss Redding."

"Lieutenant Habre." I pulled out a chair opposite her. The gentle warmth of the stone mosaic tabletop soaked into my forearms. "How are you?"

She shook her head. "I spent last night and this morning running from department to department. The research teams… did not take it well."

I sniffed. "I know that. Let me guess—they're annoyed that you think their research might possibly be causing trouble."

"I would even say affronted."

That shawarma smelled delectable, literally making my mouth water. I had to swallow before I could speak. "That's pretty usual. I've butted heads with researchers more than once, in places not a tenth this nice."

"I did get the interest of Sonny Tamara from Astrophysics, however."

I perked up. "Did he recognize the pattern?"

"No, but he did verify your mathematics."

"Great." I'd eaten, but the shawarma's garlic aroma evoked a grumble just short of a howl from my stomach. "I'm glad I didn't produce garbage."

Habre gave half a smile and glanced over at the chef a few meters away. I saw her debate the politeness of another useless offer and, thankfully, decide against it. "He did comment that he could present the data in a more usable manner."

"Please." I had to swallow before I could go on. The rich smells of the forbidden Congolese cooking were pure torture. "With mathematical analysis, I'm like a toddler playing with blocks. If one of your people can turn my numbers into a nice graph correlating the victims with the station's position, better still."

"I doubt we're that lucky." Habre reached for her glass and drew a long sip of thick mango nectar.

I tried not to stare.

"He hasn't produced anything useful yet," Habre said, putting the glass back. She gave an exhausted sigh. "Really, I should have come to tell you, but…"

"I get it," I said. "A datalink message would have been fine."

Habre rolled her eyes. "You deserve better than that."

"I deserve an extra month at that rainforest resort," I said. "With a hunky cabana boy dedicated to bringing me shrimp cocktails and another to rub my feet. What I'm going to get, though, is another forty-six days to help you sort this out before I start training to inspect tritium canisters."

"Canister inspection?" Habre said.

"Someone has to make sure nothing unpleasant gets through to Earth," I said.

"That seems… menial for you."

"I'm not exactly senior Montague security," I said. "And it's vital work. Earth needs the tritium, and it needs safety." *That's why we have Palmer here,* I added silently.

"Still," Habre said. "You're doing mathematical analysis here, and next you'll be looking at fuel tanks."

"You have to be the best to work for Montague," I said.

"And here," Habre said.

"I'm sure," I said, looking around. "Building all this must have been a nightmare."

Habre smiled. "Ask one of the engineers, they'll tell you very exciting tales." Her eyes took on a speculative look. "There's one you should talk to—perhaps a year older than you, but very knowledgeable and conscientious. From a wonderful family, excellent prospects."

Is she trying—she is*! She's trying to set me up.* I wasn't sure if I should be annoyed or flattered. "Sometime I'll do that. But right now, I'd like to make sure your people are safe before I have to move on."

Habre studied me. "You just aren't happy unless you're moving on, are you?"

She really was worried about me. "It's not that," I said. "I just… I grew up wanting to see everything. I mean, look at this." I waved a hand. "I'm in an actual space station, equipped with a fully functional pig farm, chicken ranch, and swimming pool, built to study how the Big Bang turned into our universe. This is utterly—amazing!"

Habre beamed.

"Some of the jobs, yeah—tritium inspection isn't thrilling. But there are universes out there just as amazing as this. I can't just stay home when the whole multiverse is jumping up and down, screaming 'look at me!'"

"I can understand that." Habre stabbed her fork into a notably succulent-looking chunk of shawarma. "But what about family?"

"I have a great family," I said. "I visit my folks every time I'm back on Earth."

"Visit." Habre took a bite, chewing with less relish than the dish deserved. "You're a sensible, dedicated person. You deserve better than a visit."

"Deserve again."

"Haven't you ever thought of a family? Or a life without all those silly regulations you endure?"

"Sure," I said. "But there's a whole bunch of universes out there."

Habre gave me a little sad smile. "Just so you know, there are other ways to live. Ways you could live, if you chose. I'd be happy to help you find them."

I gave her a puzzled look. "Wait—are you trying to *hire* me?"

One of Habre's shoulders lifted in a half shrug. "Hire? No. But there's a whole world on Earth too. And a few months here, a few months there—how can you build a life worth having that way?"

"I do know," I said slowly, "that if I didn't grab these chances to see everything right now, I'd regret it the rest of my life."

"Still," Habre said. "If you ever change your mind, reach out to me."

"That I can do," I said, leaning back with relief.

I couldn't imagine changing my mind—but a month ago, I couldn't imagine being in a space station.

Habre reached for her glass, and I eagerly reached for a new topic. "I'm guessing that none of your researchers recognized the pattern."

"Most dismissed it as garbage." Habre's flicker of annoyance switched to tired resignation as her datalink buzzed. A glance at the datalink, though, and I caught a flash of distress or fear or anger before she slid disciplined stillness into place.

"What is it?" I said.

"Another breakdown," she said. "Down in Ring One."

23

The concentric rings of Wemm Station got their faux gravity through rotation. Ring Two had Earth normal gravity, Ring Three a little less, all the way up to near weightlessness of Ring Six and the Hub.

The station needed a lot of supporting equipment, though. And some of it, like the magnetic field generators, needed to be mounted on the outermost part of the station. Some of those generators sluiced reactor fuel from the torrent of hydrogen screaming past us. Others produced the magnetic fields that shielded the rest of Wemm Station from the hard radiation that accompanied the hydrogen storm. A lot of that noisy, dangerous, delicate equipment was a terrible neighbor for an elementary school or your uncle's kebab stand.

Ring One housed all that gear, plus the main fusion reactors, the fabricators and their stock storage, waste recycling, the main oxygen exchangers, all the things that made the other Rings both inhabitable and worth living in. Shut down that equipment, and the rest of Wemm Station could support maybe thirty people. People who didn't care about terrible lighting, noxious smells, icky water, or slow-roasted chromosomes. The Portal would still run—all the energy it needed came from Earth, it would keep going forever unless someone took a hammer to the electrodes.

None of that gear cared about one and a third gravities. Most of it was fully automatic, so the only people who went down there were hard-core engineers supervising repairs and maintenance.

I stood up so fast my chair fell over backwards. "Ring One? Let's go."

Habre was already on her feet, her nibbled shawarma forgotten. "I'm going. You stay up here."

"Wait a minute!" I said. "I'm the liaison—"

"Exactly," Habre said. "Your boss was correct. You could have died bringing Monard in, and you have not had the training needed for high-gravity operations."

"Let's argue jurisdiction later," I said, taking the first step of a dash for the elevator.

Habre grabbed my arm. Her friendliness had evaporated, leaving a stone-hard visage. "No."

Her grip yanked me to a stop, almost making me fall back.

"I understand," Habre said, "but I do not have time right now."

My jaw clamped.

Watford had hammered it into me that the Congolese had to deal with their own problems.

He'd told—thundered—at Habre more than once to handle her problems on her own.

This wasn't a Congolese problem. It was our problem.

But Watford wouldn't see it that way.

I ached to run to the elevator.

Instead, I made myself give a single sharp nod.

Habre flashed that smile again, then was running flat-out for the closest elevator.

I flung myself down in her abandoned chair, scowling at the half-ripe grapes dangling from the vine-covered awning, Habre's abandoned wonderful-smelling shawarma, at the young hand-holding couple at a table a few meters away. They quickly looked back to their meal, speaking French in low tones.

But I could guess who they were discussing.

This was a totally useless assignment. I would be more productive inspecting tritium canisters for shipment back to Earth. At least there, if something horrible happened, I'd be permitted and expected to charge in and help.

I should set both my datalinks to count down the seconds until I got to leave this place.

And the next time Montague Human Resources offered me a surprise assignment, I'd check it really closely for stupidity.

I yanked out my Montague datalink. "Redding to Watford."

Watford said, "—hang on a minute. Watford here, Redding."

I swallowed bile. "Another mental breakdown in Ring One. Habre refuses assistance."

"Good!" Watford said. "You're making progress. If further difficulties arise, advise me and proceed to intervene. But give them the chance to settle their disputes themselves."

It's not a dispute, it's a problem. A serious problem. "Acknowledged."

"Keep me updated. Watford out."

I shoved the datalink back onto my belt.

I itched to get on my feet. Grab a high-gee suit and get to work. I hadn't practiced with a high-gee suit, but I'd read the manual.

My fists clenched.

Habre was right.

Movement in high gravity required skills I didn't have. It was no less difficult than learning to move in low gravity, except for the part where even a moment of bad balance meant breaking a bone.

My logical brain admitted that truth, while my guts screamed for me to move.

I snatched my datalinks. The Montague datalink had access to surveillance cameras, while Habre had given me access to the Congolese security feeds in the other.

But I couldn't just turn them up in the rec room, where oblivious couples flirted and a couple of toddlers chased a young beagle. (A beagle? In space?)

I jumped to my feet and stalked off.

24

My Montague datalink directed me to an unused temporary office, yet another stupid small space with a stupid keyboard and a stupidly high chair. Once there, I hit the Congolese datalink, and brought up the voice feed. The automatic translation would rob the conversation of its character, but at least I'd know what was going on.

"—tant six clear," someone said. The voice was muffled, probably by the high-gee suit.

"Octant seven clear." Another muffled but somehow familiar voice—Ramazani?

"Octant eight clear," added a third.

"Evacuation complete," Habre said. "Engineer DeKalb is down here somewhere. Continue the search."

I tasted the acid burning in my gut, and brought up security camera footage on the biggest wall. Habre surely had people in Wemm Station's security office doing the same, but another pair of eyes wouldn't hurt. Looming machines, separated by spacious corridors to accommodate the balloon-like high-gee suits. Pipes and panels and textured steel deck plates, with railings and handholds everywhere. The high-gee suits helped, but we needed every scrap of support when working at a third again normal weight.

Flip to another camera. A rubber-sheathed chain-link fence separated the walkway from a massive machine sheathed in blue ceramic and studded with dials and readouts and levers, like something from second millennium speculative movie. Much of Ring One had manual controls in addition to the automation, so that the station could be started up even if the datacore blew out. Everything had stark labels, in French.

I told the datalink to show me cameras in succession, prioritizing cameras that had not been accessed for the longest time. Soon I was studying a new scene every two seconds, countless greasy gears and acres of shining chrome and kilometers of textured steel deck.

The view flipped to a new scene just as my brain triggered on something. "Wait—go back one and hold."

The projection flicked back one camera.

The wall displayed a sprawling array of racked, exposed electronics, circuit boards connected with looping coils of wire. Text scrolled over a display, while other indicators flickered and danced in the glare of ceiling lights.

But sticking out behind the rack…

I touched the Congolese datalink. "Lieutenant Habre. Camera one-six-four-two, there's a foot sticking out behind an equipment rack. It just wiggled."

As I watched, the bulbous shape of the high-gee suit twitched again, then slid out of sight.

"Aaliyah, Pace," Habre said. "Converge on that location. Mister Diamond, what is that?"

"External Wemm field controller," said a gruff voice, like an old man who'd breathed too much smoke and dust in his life. "That's where we scoop hydrogen out of the environment."

"What can he do with it?" Habre said.

"If he shuts us down, we have enough for three, maybe four weeks. Plenty of time to bring a backup controller on-line."

"Excellent. Mary, Louis, did you hear that?" Habre said.

Two voices acknowledged.

I held the camera in place. Maybe this would end peacefully.

Moments later, two figures encased in balloon-like high-gee suits lumbered into view. Both took short, careful steps, to maintain their balance. The suits concealed even the faces—a high-gravity fall without protection could shatter someone's nose, jaw, cheekbones, or worse.

My jaw clenched in sympathetic tension.

I should be down there.

Even if the smart fabric covering the high-gee suits were decorated like an overinflated zebra and a—was that a *koala*?

The zebra lifted a small black block in one hand. "Suit deactivation chip ready."

"Go," Habre said.

"Joseph," the zebra said, shuffling towards the far end of the rack, away from where the foot had been. "Joe DeKalb. It's okay. It's just me, Louis. Louis Brittain. You remember me, friend?"

I couldn't breathe.

The zebra stepped around the rack. "Hello, Joseph."

Light flared, so brilliant I had to close my eyes and turn away.

A voice shouted in pain.

My hands clenched into fists.

The display went dark.

"Louis!" Habre shouted. "Mary! Report!"

"Suit damaged," a woman said.

Deliberately unknotting my hands, I tapped the datalink, blinking away the glare's afterimage, searching for another camera with eyes on the scene.

"We've lost telemetry from both of you," Habre said.

"Trying to back out—*oof!*"

"Mary!" Habre shouted. "What is happening?"

I heard a pained breath. "Belvie… the suit, it has failed. I've fallen. I can't see. And—and—"

"Team eight converging," someone said.

"Team two," another added.

"Lie on your back and push yourself away," Habre said. "Push with your legs."

Mary's voice sounded thick and slurred. "I can't feel my legs."

Broken back? Damaged spine?

I stood rigid. Still unable to breathe.

"Get her out of there," Habre said.

"Team eight, almost there."

Ring One wasn't just the outermost ring—it was the longest. I imagined a security team hurrying in those mincing high-gravity-safe steps.

Or running, taking the risk of a bone-breaking fall.

My lungs heaved for a single breath, then froze again.

My clenched fingers dug into the top of the chair.

When had I grabbed the chair?

"Help is coming, Mary," Habre said.

Mary huffed for breath. "I'm—I'm—"

The wall lit up again as the datalink found a camera.

I was looking down a steel-plated corridor. Black streaks scorched the walls. My eyes needed a moment to realize that the twitching mass at the end of the corridor was a half-melted high-gee suit, its occupant still trying to get the strength to work her arms.

Tension rippled through me.

The deranged DeKalb shuffled into view.

His high-gee suit looked intact, but the smart cloth displayed constantly flickering splashes of color like a bucket of broken rainbows. Each small step had the same looping, swooping manner I'd seen in Tansi and Monard.

One arm cradled a high-intensity plasma cutter. A construction tool, meant to slice through metal in a vacuum.

DeKalb took a step towards the downed Mary Tancer.

Forget protocol.

I tapped the Montague datalink. "Watford. I'm going in."

And lurched towards the door.

25

Make haste—but *slowly.*

One minute to think is better than ten minutes recovering from a screw-up.

Or a missed opportunity.

I drew up short at the loaner office's door, popped the earpiece out of the Congolese datalink, and slipped it in. The voices became tinny, but comprehensible.

"Team Eight, pull back!"

Someone screamed.

My pounding heart felt big enough to bust through the ribs caging it.

I burned to dash for the nearest elevator, but that would bring me down about a quarter of the way around Ring One from DeKalb. I needed to be closer—no, I'd move slowly in the high gravity, I couldn't possibly catch up.

I needed to get to where DeKalb was going—but before him.

Think, Redding! What do we *know*?

Baring my teeth, I swirled and grabbed my Montague datalink. It couldn't access the room's displays through the security filters, but it could project an engineering overview of Wemm Station on the wall. Fortunately, a two-dimensional spread of the six concentric rings, the Hub, and their interconnecting spokes and protruding equipment masts didn't need real-def. I could get better visuals with the Congolese datalink, but I didn't know their data as well.

And right now, only data mattered.

Data, and making the right assumptions.

There's a pattern to the madness. An unfamiliar pattern, a pattern not even the mathematicians or researchers have seen before, but a pattern.

Assume the pattern means something.

If the victim's movements and attacks are random, there's no way to figure it out. So assume their motions mean something.

The need to move quivered my every muscle. The room felt confining, the air stale, my back repulsively sweaty.

Push all that away.

Assume that all the victims are compelled, drawn, pushed to some point. A research lab? Someone's pet ferret?

Doesn't matter. Call it X.

Draw some lines, let X mark the spot.

Doctor Tansi had fired a laser from the Hub down one of the access tubes, straight towards the lower Rings. I hadn't known Wemm Station at the time well enough to guess where he was aiming. I brought up the incident report and had the laser's path sketched onto the diagram.

A little red line.

I extended the line.

Assume he was aiming at *something*.

Now Monard. When it struck he'd been on the scaffolding stretching out of the Hub, the axis to Wemm Station's spin. But he'd chosen to climb down Spoke Five.

I didn't need to draw a second line.

The red line of Tansi's hypothetical laser stretched straight down Spoke Five.

I added the location of the camera I'd been watching.

DeKalb was in Octant Eight, almost under Spoke Eight.

But he'd turned towards the camera.

Towards the point where Spoke Five hit Ring One.

That was my X.

If I took the nearest elevator down to Ring One, running to Spoke Five in one-point-three gravities would take forever.

Up here, it was a five-minute jog.

Or one minute in a tram car.

I opened the office door on a ridiculously muscular young man. His booth, right next to the office door, seemed set up for shoulder massages. He no more opened his mouth to make me an offer I wouldn't want to refuse when I bolted past him, almost tripped over a pair of toddlers, and plowed through the crowded hall towards the tram.

The tram's where I stripped off my clothes.

26

No, I'm not into recreational nudity.

But you can't wear anything under a high-gee suit. Not unless you want it to be squeezed permanently into your skin.

The tram entrances were right next to the elevators. The people at the crowded Spoke Five interchange marketplace barely had time to notice my bony rear streaking across the hall, two datalinks clutched in one hand, before the

Montague elevator slid open for me. Someone asked if I was all right amidst a couple of surprised shouts, then the doors slid shut.

As I'd told the datalink, the elevator's supply hatch popped open as the main doors shut behind me. I ignored the first aid kits, the stun guns, the restraints, and grabbed the soft gray cube of a Montague high-gee suit.

The Congolese would know me by my drabness, at least.

I'd read the manual, but hadn't ever used a suit before.

The elevator dinged for instructions.

"Hold in place," I said. The cube felt soft but weirdly heavy, like foam padding around a block of gold. "Engage high-gee suit."

The cube twitched in my hand.

Right. When the manual says don't wear anything, they mean *anything*. I tugged my earpiece out, slipped it back into the Congolese datalink, and set both datalinks on the ground.

The cube shimmered and slumped, then started oozing up my arm.

The plastic felt clean and soft, almost cottony. The sight of the plastic crawling up my skin should have made me feel kind of uneasy, the way it looked like an old movie monster devouring my flesh. Instead, I only felt impatient at how slowly it moved. I needed to be downstairs *now*.

When the plastic hit my chest a few seconds later, though, it spread in every direction simultaneously. I felt it slither across my shoulder blades, down my spine, over my breasts. I couldn't prevent a nervous twitch as the suit slid smoothly up my neck. Suddenly, its inexorable movement wasn't too slow—it seemed too fast, rising over the point of my chin and cradling my ears.

I involuntarily sucked a deep breath.

The suit oozed over my chin—

—and stopped just brushing my lower lip.

Plastic still flowed downward, clamping my buttocks together, softly but implacably squeezing my thighs, my shins.

More plastic oozed up the crown of my head, over my forehead, halting just short of my eyes.

I released my breath. The suit shifted with my ribs, maintaining its intimately close contact.

I suddenly felt aware of a chill around my feet, clammy on the metal deck. What had the manual said?

Right. I grabbed the elevator's hand rail with one hand and lifted a foot.

The plastic slithered south, encasing that foot.

When I switched feet, I found the suit had added five centimeters to my height. Padding and reinforcement for my soon-to-be-abused arches.

Once my feet were covered, the suit inflated.

The cotton grip on my legs turned hard, plush over steel. The squeezing had a rhythm, though. A rippling pulse, just slightly out of synch with my own heart.

My heart would have to work extra hard to get blood out of those extremities. The suit monitored my blood flow, squeezing my legs like a toothpaste tube, coaxing spent blood back to my lungs.

I bent to grab my datalinks.

The suit's spine locked up, from my shoulders to my tailbone.

Bending over in high gravity was a good way to fall on your face and break a bone. The suit knew I was in normal gravity, but it already enforced proper high-gee behavior.

The extra weight and strain of high gravity was a problem, but most people could handle an extra thirty percent for a short time. But the reflexes, the muscle memory, the habits: those things would maim you. Bend forward too quickly when your head and shoulders weighed too much, and gravity would send you straight to the deck. Headfirst. You could hop, but you'd come down too quickly and probably break your toes. Pull something off a high shelf? It would be too heavy, and plummet too quickly.

Every little motion transformed into a way for your lifelong habits to harm you.

I bent at my knees, fumbling for the datalinks. It felt like I was wearing heavy gloves, but the suit easily picked up the datalinks and let me slap them at opposite sides of my waist, where the datalink clips should be. The suit had no clips, but the plastic formed cradles at a touch.

My astonishment at how easily that worked only drove home that I had no training for this. Zero. I'd never worn a high-gee suit before, let alone spent time in high gravity.

Unfamiliar equipment?

Dangerous, alien environment?

No training, no practice, but straight into the disaster?

A great way to get killed.

I brushed my fingers over the Congolese datalink. Tried to brush, at least—my fingers felt an extra centimeter long. I managed to engage the voice commands and bring up the voice channel to Habre's team. The Congolese datalink couldn't access the Montague suit's voice circuits, but the suit relayed the sounds for me.

"I could take him," a masculine voice said.

"Not in that area," Habre said. "The equipment's too delicate. Engineer Roundtree says section twelve, Octant Six."

"He's moving too quickly," the voice said.

"Maxwell, you may not override your suit!" Habre said.

"But—" The man sounded furious. "Yes, Lieutenant."

"Team six? Can you get to section twelve before Joseph?"

"Yes," said another man.

Habre said, "Wait for him to pass. Ambush him with the shutdown chip. Team Five, move to Octant Six, section… four. If the ambush fails, you're authorized to use deadly force. Remember, no matter what, no physical contact."

Good. Touching Monard had been a disaster. Habre was assuming that touching this new victim would be as disastrous. Living in high gravity is easier than living in vacuum, but a sudden withdrawal of the high-gee suit would unbalance anyone.

And unbalance meant you'd break only a dozen bones. With luck.

But at least it sounded like the area at the bottom of Spoke Five wasn't a war zone. Yet.

I tried to say *elevator*, but all that came out was a strangled grunt.

My jaw wouldn't open. The suit held it in place.

I pulled in a deep breath. "Elevator," I said through gritted teeth, suddenly sounding a lot more like Habre and her people. "Ring One."

My weight dropped with the elevator.

I'd be a lot heavier soon.

27

The elevator had hardly started when Habre said, "Miss Redding, what are you doing?"

My Congolese datalink had betrayed my motions. I couldn't have prevented it if I'd wanted to. "Watford told me to intervene if the situation warranted it. People are dying. It's warranted."

"We don't have a chip thrower for you," Habre said.

"I don't know what a chip thrower is, so that's fine," I said.

It's really hard to sound calm and collected when your teeth are held clenched by a semi-intelligent high-gee suit.

"Miss Redding, stay clear of the struggle," Habre said. "Team Six, are you in position?"

"Almost."

"You have four minutes until DeKalb arrives," Habre said.

"We'll make it."

The moment of lightness from the elevator starting its plunge passed. I suddenly felt worryingly heavy, like I'd really overdone the carbs at a resort's all-you-can-gorge buffet. My guts seemed to droop low, my heart throbbing extra hard. The suit sent ripples of pressure up my legs, and the foam beneath my feet felt a whole lot firmer.

The elevator moved slowly between Ring Two and Ring One, giving people time to acclimate. My knees creaked, sending dull flashes of pain up to join the aches where the bones of my spine started compressing my disks. The pressure of the suit squeezing back was almost worse, as it tried to hoist my ribs into the air. The suit didn't keep my jaw shut to keep it from falling down—it used my jaw to keep my skull at the top of my neck.

I've felt more unpleasant sensations while working for Montague.

But I'd have to sit down and figure out where exactly this fit in my top five.

My pulse sounded overly loud and rapid in my ears.

The elevator glided to a smooth, gentle halt, and the doors slid open.

I took a step towards the drab steel chamber outside.

Or, I tried to.

The suit stiffened up, not allowing me to move.

What had the manual said? Right: half steps. Crouch, don't bend.

With conscious care, I shuffled my right foot forward. It slid maybe half my normal stride before the suit started pushing back.

I shifted my weight to that foot and dragged the other forward.

In mincing half-steps, I eased my way out of the elevator and into the corridor.

While the Congolese had gone over all the upper layers of Wemm Station like an interior decorator with too much time on his hands, the Ring One antechamber had no furnishings or décor beyond the purely functional. It looked almost Montague in its starkness. Light panels welded to overhead girders cast soft illumination across pipes and systems. We might have mostly autonomous electronics and smart fabric pressure suits, but when it comes to heavy lifting like moving large amounts of water and air or sifting hydrogen from the void, nothing beats good old-fashioned dedicated-purpose machinery. Every device featured quaint mechanical controls, for emergencies. The cool harsh air stank of electricity and industrial grease.

Not to mention the cosmic rays shooting through here. Ring One was outside the magnetic shields that protected the crew.

My stomach flopped at the thought.

To the left and right, long corridors curved upwards with the Ring. No matter where I walked, centripetal force would make it look like I was at the bottom of a wheel. The effect wasn't so obvious in the crowded, busy corridors of the upper Rings, but the empty clear corridor and the dreadful heaviness made the artificiality more obvious and oppressive.

"We are in position," the Team Six spokesman said in my ear.

"Excellent," Habre said. "Autumn, at your discretion."

Next to the elevators, a plain steel door bore a label of SPOKE 5 ENGINEERING OFFICE. Broad arrows marked the directions to OCTANT SIX and OCTANT FOUR.

I turned towards Six and started shuffling.

By the time I covered a few meters, I'd gotten the hang of the mincing gait needed to walk in high gravity. Knees bent just a little. Feet splayed out a few extra degrees. Place each foot ten, maybe fifteen centimeters in front of the other. Spine straight.

Each breath made my lungs ache. The high-gee suit squeezed my abs with each exhalation, adding their strength to my strained diaphragm. I wasn't sure if the pressure really helped, or if the suit was just trying to convince me that it helped.

Plus, frustration made my blood seethe.

Ring One was almost a kilometer and a quarter around. That made each octant, what? A hundred fifty meters? If each of my steps was ten centimeters, I needed fifteen hundred steps to get to Octant Six, another fifteen hundred to Octant Seven.

The suit wasn't the only reason my teeth were gritted.

On camera, DeKalb had moved a lot faster than me.

Too soon I heard, "Team Six reporting. Here he comes."

I should be there.

Why had I wasted time charting random garbage, when I could have just gone down Spoke Six where everything was happening?

Habre said, "Great luck, Samuel."

"I don't need luck, Belvie. I have a great plan and a seriously great partner."

"Shush," said a new voice.

"Sam. Madonna," Habre said. "Mind on the job."

I itched to have the datalink bring up visuals from the camera, but with this painfully heavy machine-assisted gait I didn't need the distraction.

Surely they had carts around here? Some kind of electric scooter for quicker travel? The corridor was wide enough. I'd have to keep my eyes open for one, or for a Ring tram stop.

Instead, I moved as quickly as the suit permitted. The added weight sucked at my soul.

"Almost there," the Team Six spokesman hissed.

I tensed.

The suit shortened my steps even further to compensate.

The remainder of Habre's team held silence.

I fought to relax, to move more quickly.

"Got him!" shouted the Team Six lead, Samuel. "Malware engaged—"

His voice came apart in a scream. Static filled the channel.

Then silence.

Except for Habre shouting for her people to answer.

Heart pounding, I tapped my Montague datalink.

Watford's voice instantly sounded in my ear. "Redding. You may not override the suit's safety circuits."

I muted the Congolese datalink. "Habre just lost a team."

"I saw," Watford said. "But you lack the training to use the suit at a higher speed. We are *not* losing you too."

"These people are not expendable!" I shouted.

"Even if you get up there," he said, "what are you going to do against a plasma cutter?"

I shook, and not just from the physical strain. Anger burned a pit in my stomach. "Something. We can't just stand by," I gasped. The suit made me take a breath before I could finish.

Watford cut me off. "I have an armed squad trained for high-gee operations assembling near Spoke Six. They'll be down in ninety seconds, with chaff guns and laser rifles. DeKalb isn't getting past them."

"Habre has a team between Spoke Six and DeKalb," I said.

"Percival has them falling back now to join our people," Watford said. "They will fire on Habre's command."

His calm, intense voice only frustrated me more. Even though I couldn't possibly get far enough ahead quickly enough, I fought to relax my legs and swing my legs a little faster, a little further. The suit fought my every effort.

I could just turn the suit off. Peel it away, walk without protection.

The corridor had handrails. They would help.

Trip once, try to catch my weight on my arms, and shatter them both before flattening my nose.

I let my hands curl into fists. "Yes, sir."

But I didn't stop shuffling forward.

"Just in case, sir," I said. "If that fails…"

"Yes, Redding?" Watford sounded annoyed now.

I couldn't believe I was saying this. "Maybe you better send Palmer down here to join me."

28

I'd shuffled another twenty tedious meters between complicated machines down Ring One's main corridor when I heard soft footsteps behind me. The bulky suit did let me turn my head, and when I spread my feet and bent a knee I could even shift at the waist to look over my shoulder.

Palmer.

He'd stripped out of his uniform, leaving himself clad only in that body stocking of loosely meshed translucent blue plastic and a barely adequate sky-blue thong. The finger-sized gaps in the plastic mesh framed the weirdly regular freckle-sensors covering his whole body.

His body didn't seem to make any concessions to the extra gravity other than a slight bend in the knee. That perfect musculature didn't sag. His cheeks didn't even droop.

I couldn't help wondering about Palmer. Just how much of the guy was still meat, anyway? And what would make someone choose that sort of dehumanizing augmentation? He always seemed cheerful, but what was really going on in his head?

"Redding," Palmer said, trotting up easily, bare feet padding on the metal deck.

I habitually tried to nod. The bulky high-gee suit prevented the motion, triggering a strain in the back of my neck. "Palmer." I faced forward again and took a short, suit-supported, suit-restrained step. "Good of you to join us."

"I like playing clean-up," Palmer said, slowing down to pace me. "It means someone else handled everything before I got there." His tone was light, but his narrow eyes looked intent.

"Must be nice," I said. "Getting other people to do all the work."

"I have gotten pretty good at Go on this assignment," Palmer said.

"I never understood that game," I said, shuffling forward.

"Once our teammates handle this kerfuffle, let's take an evening and I'll explain it to you."

"Here he comes," Habre said in my ear.

I held up a hand for silence, but Palmer was already nodding.

"Stun guns ready," Habre said in my ear.

"If this goes badly," Palmer said quietly, "I'm going ahead. That cross-corridor ahead is a good spot for an ambush. You hang back and wait for instructions."

A spectator again. Great. "Understood."

"Hold," Habre said.

I made myself breathe.

"Fire."

The audio dissolved into a thin crackle. Interference from the electrical stun guns.

Despite myself, I paused. The fight was happening right now, and I wasn't there. In a few seconds, once they secured DeKalb, I'd turn around and shuffle back to the elevator. Or Palmer would get his chance.

The crackle faded.

Silence.

"Everyone." Habre sounded ill. "Fire at will."

This time, I heard the sound even around the rising curve of Ring One. A bone-deep buzz traveled through the steel deck and up into my teeth, making my eyeballs shiver in their sockets.

I couldn't help a grimace. Montague laser rifles could burn through a high-gee suit and the person inside them without trouble. The chaff guns would shred a plastic suit and gnaw the meat off the person inside.

Right now, I could imagine Habre's grim expression as she watched people cut down one of her people. Watford should have given the order to fire, taken that burden—no, that would be harder for Habre to live with.

Maybe.

Did Habre know DeKalb? Were they related?

Habre spoke often of her affection for her family, for her husband. I scrabbled to recall his name, sick it might be Joe? No—Lincoln, that was it.

Even so, Wemm Station wasn't that big. She knew DeKalb, just as she'd known Tansi and Monard.

Was that scream over the datalink pain? Anger?

Impatience made me tremble.

My Montague datalink relayed, "Percival reporting. DeKalb is down."

"Dead?" Watford said.

"With what's left?" Percival said. "I certainly hope so, sir."

"Watch him anyway," Watford ordered.

"Assuming nothing, sir," Percival said.

Tension ran out of me like water from a burst balloon. I suddenly felt exhausted, both physically and even spiritually. We'd fought to keep Monard alive, and the Congolese physicians hadn't been able to rebuild his brain. Our people had killed DeKalb—and maybe he was the better off of the two.

"Well," Palmer said, "another exciting day where I do nothing at all. Look me up later, we'll have a stab at Go."

"Thanks."

"Palmer," Watford said, "Redding hasn't yet taken high-gee training. Get her back to the elevator, please."

"I can make it," I said, even as Palmer said, "Acknowledged."

"Fine," I said. "Watch me."

"That's not what Watford said."

"Then what?"

"Hold still."

"He said leave."

Impossibly quick, Palmer crouched beside me and deftly scooped me off the floor.

My suit immediately shifted its focus, providing firm supports for my back and legs. The neck firmed, cradling my head up.

I squawked in outrage, free arm flailing. "You put me down!"

"Orders," Palmer said, barely hiding a grin.

I was *not* letting Palmer carry me back to the elevator. That video would make the rounds faster than me throwing myself into deep space.

"I don't care what your orders are!" The suit didn't let me swing very hard, but I still bopped Palmer on the temple with a foam-suited hand.

Palmer stopped trying to hide the smile. "I'm not going against Watford's orders."

Worse—my clothes were still in the tram. I'd been in such a hurry to get down here, I hadn't thought about keeping any dignity on my way out.

And Palmer was the closest one could get to naked and not get arrested.

The two of us, stark naked, getting off the elevator together? They'd would put *that* video on loop in the cafeteria seven nights a week.

No, I'd keep the high-gee suit on. Hobble through Ring Three to the Montague locker room.

I hadn't helped at all with this crisis, and now Palmer was stripping the rest of my dignity away. "Stop enjoying this!"

"I wouldn't enjoy this nearly so much if you weren't so outraged," he said.

My best swing at him was like a newborn taking a swipe at her mother.

I made myself settle down, fuming. Hopefully, my face hadn't gotten too much redder.

The best I could hope for was boring video.

I couldn't *wait* to start inspecting tritium shipments.

I had another minute or so to practice my self-control before Habre said, "Oh, no."

The station rocked around us.

29

Wemm Station weighed over a million tons.

It shook like a child's rattle.

Somehow, Palmer held his balance on the deck and kept me in his arms.

My puffy high-gee suit turned stiff around my ears, protecting them from the eruption of sound. I felt it, though—the air itself shook and quivered, rippling through the suit, vibrating my teeth against each other, making my bones shudder against every joint and muscle.

I'm pretty sure I tried to scream, but the high-gee suit didn't let me open my mouth or breathe deeply enough.

The brutal shaking faded slowly, like an angry deity had used a cosmic sledgehammer to ring Wemm Station like a bell.

I needed a moment to orient myself.

Palmer hadn't stayed upright. When the world had rocked around us…

…he'd dropped to one knee.

Still holding me steady.

Somehow that made him more human—and more impressive.

"Are you all right?" Palmer asked.

"Yes," I said. "Thanks."

Palmer glanced up and down the service corridor. "Heavy infrared from spinward—Spoke Six."

My heart quivered. I triggered both datalinks. "Habre? Percival?"

No answer.

A weird triple beep sounded in both ears, almost simultaneously. I needed a moment to recognize it.

Both datalinks, cut off from the network.

What had *happened*?

The lighting flickered—not all at once, but in a ripple, darkness flashing down the corridor, past us, disappearing up the curve of Ring One.

That wasn't right. Power failure, sure. But a power failure that *moved*?

I had a sick feeling that while this universe might be mathematically identical to our own, its natural laws might not be.

And they'd just turned on us.

30

Still reeling from the concussion that shook Wemm Station, my brain wobbling in my skull, I managed to ask, "Do you have any signal?"

Palmer answered by leaping straight from kneeling on the textured metal deck into a run, straight between machinery back towards Spoke Five.

His legs pounded incredibly hard beneath me, as if he was an Olympic sprinter on Earth rather than in Ring One's unnaturally high gravity. Somehow, the pounding didn't rock me—I could have been lying atop a slab of bedrock for all the motion he passed through to me.

"Network is down." Palmer actually sounded a little short of breath. "Unnatural vibration in the Ring. Get up the Spoke, I'm going back to check."

"Not alone you're not!" I said.

"You can't help me," Palmer said. "You can do the most good aiding the evacuation."

The answer stopped me.

I imagined the panicked chaos right now in Ring Two. Damaged lighting, air tainted with smoke or chemicals or just plain old carbon dioxide. Screaming children, terrified parents.

How many people had that blast injured?

What systems had failed?

The high-gee suit could protect me from fire, from air turned toxic or outright missing, but the people over us had no such protections.

Bile burned in my gut.

Was there even a Ring Two any more?

Palmer was right. We'd have to get everyone up to Ring Three, into the Portal. Trigger the evacuation protocol.

The two laughing children who'd played hide-and-peek around my knees when I first saw Ring Two flashed through my memory.

What if Montague decided that the evacuees had brought something back with them? If they'd carried an unknown, unknowable threat from this void? Something dangerous to the human race, to Earth?

I knew exactly "what if."

But they had a better chance on Earth, even in a Montague quarantine chamber, than on a damaged space station in an empty universe.

"This is what I'm here for," Palmer said. "This is why I exist—to go where other people can't."

Watford was right. I ran towards problems.

And here, I couldn't.

The only thing I could do was help other people flee.

"Fine!" I spat.

Everything had gone wrong, and I was *still* playing babysitter.

The lights flickered again, an unnatural band of darkness progressing from one end of the visible corridor to the other in less than a breath.

Palmer only needed a minute to return me to the Spoke Five antechamber. It seemed weirdly unchanged. I felt like the engineering office should have been burst open, or a floor plate tossed aside, or something.

No, there was a change. Small lights burned amber over all four elevators.

"Stairs," Palmer said. The stairwell door on the far side of the elevators, across from the engineering office.

Two hundred meters of stairs back to Ring Two. In a high-gee suit. They'd have the station evacuated before I got halfway up. "Right."

Palmer swung me back upright and lowered me to the floor. "Let me plug in first."

"Okay." The suit shifted to support me as I regained my feet, but my innards seemed to ooze unpleasantly against their unaccustomed weight. The network might be down, but if Palmer could access the hard-wired systems, I'd at least find out if Ring Two still existed.

Maybe Watford could direct me somewhere I could do some good.

Palmer slid a dull yellow panel to the side, exposing a small screen and a series of sockets. "Don't laugh," he said.

Before I could say *This isn't funny*, Palmer licked his pinky and cautiously slid it into one of the open sockets. Exactly like we tell children not to.

I couldn't help chuckling through gritted teeth.

"Laugh it up, Redding," Palmer said, his own teeth gritted. "This isn't as easy as it looks. Bypass… there… and—ah, there we go!"

"What's going on?" I said.

"Ruptured fluorox line blew in Ring One, Spoke Six."

My heart sagged even further.

Habre. Percival.

Everyone there, lost.

Palmer had his eyelids closed, but the eyes beneath twitched as his optical implants fired. "Monitors show structural damage to that part of the Ring. Magnetic shields and hydrogen scoop both down. Network is live on Ring Two and above. Commander Mvouba has ordered preparation for evacuation, but not full evac yet. Watford wants you up in Ring Three as soon as possible, to handle comms with the Congolese."

I remembered the last time Watford had talked directly with Mvouba, and felt certain it wasn't going any better this time. "I'm on my way," I said, resigned.

The worst part of your own helplessness?

Being helpless against it.

Palmer gave a brief nod to acknowledge my words. "You're not to override your suit's safeties until you're within fifty meters of Ring Two. I'll check the blast site, and follow you," Palmer said. His mouth twisted in concentration. "Just trying the backup cameras... hmm... There's some weird kind of ... interference?"

The ring of flickering lights flowed towards us.

Horrified realization ripped through me.

The world slowed down.

Trying to get the words out, my brain felt just as slow.

I shouted "Disconnect!" fearing, *knowing*, I was too late.

Palmer didn't even acknowledge what I said before the dim lighting hit us.

The ring of shadow stopped, right over us.

Palmer's feet jittered on the deck like he'd touched live voltage, but the rest of his body didn't move. His silent mouth twitched.

Whatever was causing the lighting problems, whatever had triggered the blast, whatever had broken and maimed people—

It had Palmer.

I itched to shove Palmer away from the wall. My high-gee suit was made out of a smart fabric similar to the pressure suits, though. Touching Monard had destroyed the suit.

Instead I glanced around for a loose pipe, a hammer, any kind of tool I could use to knock Palmer away from the wall. A broom? A stick? The best I saw was a chunk of conduit that had busted its weld along two sides, but I'd need a cutting torch just to break the other two sides free.

Palmer's shoulders began to quiver.

Given a couple minutes, I could brew a decent plan.

But I only had time for a stupid one.

31

I desperately snatched the Montague datalink with one hand and the corridor's handrail with the other. This was the most foolish thing I've done yet. "Deactivate high-gee suit."

The lights around us remained dim. Palmer's chin had joined the quivering. His closed eyes bulged behind closed lids.

The stupid datalink chirped for confirmation. I barely kept from shouting as I said "Override safety protocols. Deactivate high-gee suit, maximum speed!"

If the network had been live, the suit would have contacted the Montague datacore for confirmation. Without the network, though, I had complete control.

My feet smoothly sank a couple centimeters. The smooth cottony feeling of the high-gee suit's boots faded into warm, sweaty textured steel.

The hand grabbing the rail seemed to sink, easing my bare palm into meeting the smooth, cool aluminum rail. The sweat on my hand instantly chilled.

My heart hammered in my chest.

With my contact points exposed, the suit sluiced off me like water.

One moment I'd been trapped in a terribly uncomfortable full-body stocking that squeezed me everywhere. The next, my every joint ground in protest as that support evaporated like water dancing on a griddle. My vision grayed, as if I looked at the world through a tiny round window. Everything wobbled.

Distantly, I heard both datalinks clang against the deck.

My exposed bare skin suddenly felt cool, everywhere. I could feel the grease and smoke in the air.

No time to worry about any of that.

A labored breath, and color seeped back into my vision.

Most of Palmer's body twitched now. He seemed suspended, as if someone had drilled a hole into his head and dangled him from a line. His pinky jammed in the data socket tethered him to the wall.

I heaved in a breath. My chest opened more, letting me get more air in, but my chest muscles seemed to tighten with the motion.

No time for this, I thought. I have to do this right.

And right *now*.

Keeping my knees bent a little more than usual, I took one tiny step towards Palmer. Another.

My arm felt sunk in fresh cement, but I raised it to face level.

Putting everything behind it, I punched the heel of my palm right into the killer cyborg's breastbone.

If Palmer had resisted me, I'd have had all the effect of a kitten batting a whale. Palmer didn't resist. He didn't even try to catch his balance, instead toppling straight back to smash into the deck.

But the part I cared about most, his pinky, popped right out of the socket.

The extra gravity brought him down with freakish speed and an ear-smashing clang.

Immediately, the lights around us returned to full strength.

I clutched the handrail, trying to ignore the metaphorical bags of concrete tied over my shoulders. "Palmer!" I said.

Palmer lay on his back, arms pointed straight up. An irrational, unnatural twitch rippled up and down his body.

Dread gnawed at my bones. Had the mind-destroying pattern infected him? Or would he recover?

"Palmer!" I shouted.

What if he didn't get up? Leave him here? I sure couldn't carry him up the stairs the way he could have me.

Palmer's back arched. His teeth clanged together.

Crouch and help him? No, if he bumped me in one of these seizures I'd fall. And I was infinitely more fragile than Palmer.

His hands dug into the steel deck. No, they didn't claw at it—he bent his fingers, and the floor plate dimpled beneath them.

Maybe it was best I didn't hold his hand.

"Come on, Palmer," I said.

Back still arched, Palmer hissed, "Redding."

I barely stopped myself from leaning closer. "I'm here, Palmer."

Palmer's left hand released the deck, making this weird looping swipe at the air.

The motion sent shivers down my spine.

"Security Third Redding." The inflectionless words, as if Palmer was typing the words into a primitive speech synthesizer, chilled my marrow. "Remove yourself from proximity." A thin electronic whine swelled behind his words. "Immediate. Threat. Control."

Palmer's voice spiraled into a familiar, dreadful, impossible shriek.

32

Despite the hot, muggy, and now smoky air of Ring One, despite the oppressive weight, my blood ran cold.

Palmer went limp and collapsed against the deck, hitting a fraction of a second faster than my brain insisted he should have.

I don't run away.

I haven't run away since I was, what, five?

I'd fled that schoolyard bully, then run back.

But the monotone abhuman shriek ripping out of Palmer's throat convinced me I wasn't running away.

I was running towards.

Towards living.

I spun too quickly. The world turned gray, and I felt blood leave my brain. I clutched the hand rail with both hands instead of falling, and even then planted my face against the warm metal wall. An antique-style analog gauge gouged my cheek.

I forced a deep breath.

The world returned.

Put the high-gee suit back on? No—no time.

Move. Carefully.

But quickly.

People a third heavier than I am get around without trouble. But their bodies have had time to adjust, to develop the strength and hydrostatic balance to support that mass. Dump that much weight on someone instantaneously, make gravity itself treacherously unfamiliar, and their body has trouble pushing around all those fluids. They get clumsy.

Feeble.

I fumbled forward.

In only a couple meters I found a balance. Reach forward and grab the hand rail. Move the opposite foot up to it. Step past with the other foot. Repeat, always keeping two points in contact.

Just like a one-legged person free climbing.

A one-legged person wearing a concrete overcoat.

My labored pulse thundered in my ears.

The deck's rough texture dug at my feet. I had no problem walking barefoot, I did it all the time, but not on hard steel. I had to be, what—over a hundred kilograms now? Something like that.

It wasn't just the jagged steel savaging my unprepared feet, though. The floor carried an asymmetric, irregular vibration. Not the grumble of distant motors carrying out their usual tasks. More the feeling of great gears with missing teeth, clashing against each other.

Don't be dramatic, I told myself. Ring One is not going to shake itself apart.

That vibration was probably there all along, damped by the high-gee suit.

But the thought wouldn't leave as I limped and dragged myself into motion.

The stairwell was only a few meters in front of me. At least it was on my side of the hall, not next to the elevators. Make it that far and start climbing.

I lurched forward, thinking: what then?

Palmer was the most dangerous person on Wemm Station. Montague had obviously hired him specifically to guard the facility against unknown threats. If I was the babysitter, he was the tyrannosaurus-sitter.

They'd already evacuated Ring One, even before I got down here. I'd heard Habre confirm it.

If I went up, I'd be abandoning Palmer to do—whatever it was.

Maybe he'd just make his way further down. Fling himself off the outside of Ring One. Badly confuse alien archaeologists in thirteen billion years or so.

Maybe he'd wreck some critical device doing it.

Red lights still flagged four inoperable elevators.

Sweat poured down my face.

I could already feel my feet swelling, as my heart labored to push blood against oppressive weight.

And what could I do? I was naked—literally, and metaphorically—against him.

My hand slipped an inch.

Behind me, Palmer squealed again.

I didn't dare look back.

Forward.

Climb the stairs, I told myself.

Get people out of here.

Let Palmer blow up Wemm Station if he wanted to.

But how long would an evacuation take?

And how long would it take Palmer to wreck the place?

If that's what he was going to do.

Maybe he'd sit down and squeal in place.

It could happen.

Pushing as hard as I dared, I put my hand on the stairwell doorframe more quickly than I would have guessed. I risked a quick look back.

Palmer had curled up on his side, his back to me. The arm on top flailed in wide, looping, uncoordinated circles. He bounced onto his back, thrown by his other arm. His legs swung out, like he was trying to get traction on air to walk straight up, heels clanging against the deck with a screech of bending metal.

Even if he didn't get up, his damaged brain might trigger seizures severe enough to make his ridiculously augmented body crack apart this part of Ring One.

If I was going to take action, I needed something. Knowledge of Ring One. Palmer's manual. A club, even.

I swallowed.

Only one way to get any of that. And it wasn't by climbing the stairs.

I forced my aching lungs to push themselves empty, so I could draw a fresh, smoke-tainted breath.

Peel my fingers off the handrail.

And started walking across the corridor to the Spoke Five Engineering Office.

33

If you ever have to walk in excessive gravity, bring a cane.

Two canes.

Maybe a walker. Or a powered wheelchair.

I'd gone three steps before I realized I had made a mistake.

Lifting my foot clear of the floor to take a step meant risking my balance on one leg. Even moving slowly, minor wobbles threatened to turn catastrophic. I found myself compelled to slide my feet forward, centimeters at a time.

Across textured steel.

Worst pedicure I've ever had.

My heart didn't feel like it was beating any more. It throbbed so rapidly it might as well have been shimmying. My throat ached, both from the effort and from the bitter smoke increasing in the air. If I breathed too deeply I wanted to cough, and I didn't dare. I might bend, and fall.

Slide a foot a few centimeters.

Faintest hint of a wobble? Put it back down.

Shift the other foot.

I tried holding my arms out for balance, but they felt draped with buckets of water. I had to hug them to my chest.

My eyes started watering.

The back of my throat burned.

Palmer let out this irregular warble, his voice sliding wildly up and down, occasionally hanging flat in place. An audible representation of the pattern I'd found? Or spasms from a dying brain?

My stomach clenched and knotted. I needed to relax, or I wouldn't make it.

A clock would probably say it took me a minute, maybe ninety seconds. But each of those seconds lasted at least a year.

I felt a surge of triumph as I got close enough to touch the door.

Just before I my fingers could brush the metal, though, the door slid open.

"Quick!" someone shouted. "In here."

34

The engineering office was larger than I'd expect for a room in Ring One. It's not like people would come down here to bask in a healthy one-point-three gravities for meetings.

But what caught my attention first was the big, luxurious, *beautiful* high-gee mobile chair standing like a padded monolith right inside the door.

I snatched the doorframe for balance, shuffled forward, and clamped my other hand on the chair. Heart pounding against both the gravity and anticipation, I wobbled myself in a tiny circle and stepped backwards onto the conveniently shallow footrest.

The intelligent chair instantly took over. I found myself tipping backwards, sinking into the smart foam. I groaned with pleasure as my weight came off my brutalized arches—how do heavy people even stand? The chair reformed itself so that I reclined, feet and arms raised.

I suddenly understood exactly why my father loved his recliner.

"Rest," a man with a thick Congolese accent said as my chair rolled into position next to him. He broke into a torrent of high-velocity French. A computerized voice responded. He issued more commands. On the ceiling, over to my left, display windows shuffled.

I turned my head to look up.

Dozens of graphs and status readouts filled the ceiling, positioned to easily read while lying in the chair next to me. A window flashed through camera views of the service corridor, cramped crawlspaces, narrow gaps between devices.

The man rattled more instructions in French.

The camera flashed onto a view of a hall full of broken metal. Bluish steam billowed from a shattered overhead pipe, obscuring everything, but I made out steel floor plates, ruptured upward like a monstrous plant had suddenly blossomed.

Something moved off to one side.

A hand?

The camera angle switched, looking down the service corridor, with the same blue steam billowing from behind.

"Wait!" I said. "That last shot!"

My heart was too tired to beat more quickly, but it tried. Had I really glimpsed a crawling figure?

"Yes," the man said. "Five, maybe six, still alive."

I rolled my head to the side.

The Congolese man in the chair a meter from me looked youthful, with a shaven head and heavy cheeks. He wore a mostly deflated high-gee suit. His brown eyes focused on the ceiling, even as his strong fingers danced on the keyboard on his lap. The chair had formed armrests over his stomach, letting him type lying down even with this absurd weight. "If I can shut the lube leak— shut this down…" He peered at one of the readouts. "They might stay alive." His keyboard clattered.

Almost directly overhead, a set of squiggling lines turned bright red and started oscillating wildly. Yellow indicators started flashing red.

I sucked in a clean-tasting breath to ask, but they had already slid back to yellow.

My companion said, "Yes, yes—friction, Spoke Six's blown lube. A rotation, shake. We have worse."

I deliberately stilled myself. "Can I help?"

"Yes," the man said. "Shush."

Bitter helplessness made me want to scream. Again.

Instead, I took a breath and lay still, willing my body to recover. I felt like I'd just run a half-marathon, barefoot, over gravel. Steel gravel.

In only a few seconds, the camera showed the plume of blue smoke fading.

"That's it!" he crowed. "Take that, you stupid beautiful…"

The view flipped back to the shattered pipe. Fresh smoke had stopped pluming out. The existing smoke spiraled towards the tiny air vents near the floor, more fully exposing ruptured floor plates.

My companion let out a deep breath. "That stuff, it eats through gee-suits. I'm Tove. You be the famous Miss Redding."

The abrupt conversational swerve took me by surprise. "Uh, nice to meet you, Tove. Thanks for the chair."

"Least I could." Tove peered at the ceiling, seemingly having forgotten to say the rest of the sentence. "We've stopped losing pressure."

The display above me squiggled its wild red again.

Tove's fingers clattered. "Repressurizing lube."

The squiggles faded.

I eased my breath.

Tove said, "We won't know for thirty-five seconds if that worked. Might structural damage." His eyes fixed on the squiggling lines in my part of the ceiling. "Your friend?"

"Hurt," I said. That didn't seem a big enough word to describe what happened to Palmer. And Tove's random dropping of words vastly annoyed me.

"Recirc is on, but lube eats through skin better than gee-suits."

"Can you get me a view?"

"Datalink?"

"Out in the hall."

"Right." Tove glanced at me, then jerked his eyes back to the ceiling displays. "Sorry."

Wait—was he actually blushing? "How old are you, Tove?"

His hands clattered on the keyboard. "Does it matter?"

His posture had deceived me. He couldn't even be six feet tall, short for a Congolese. His arms had the thin strength of youth. "You're someone's kid, aren't you?"

"I'm not a kid!" He heaved a hand up to point at the ceiling over my chair. "See! Friction's stopped!"

Had it been thirty-five seconds? The ceiling over me kept its steady squiggle. "Good work, Tove," I said.

"I'm not here because of my dad," Tove said.

Oh, boy. "Of course you're not." I thought carefully. "You fixed things so quickly, I just thought you were a senior engineer, that's all."

"s'nobody else," Tove said. "Something fried the engineering datacore."

"Isn't that scattered throughout the Ring?" I said.

"Supposed to!" He issued instructions in French, and the overhead displays swooped into a new configuration. These readouts had a lot more red. "I'm trying reset but no."

Red spots flashed on the ceiling.

"Dad said datacore can't fail," Tove said, his voice just a little panicked.

I wanted to tell him that this was an alien universe and anything could happen, but didn't think that would help. "Don't freak out on me, Tove. Stop and think a moment. Can you get help managing this from Ring Two?"

"Not with datacore down. They've sent some engineers down, but I can't elevators running."

Get, I thought. The word is *get*. "Where are they coming down?"

"Spoke Four." He glanced at me, but his face blushed even more strongly and he wrenched his face back to the ceiling. "Supposed to wait here."

What was he, fifteen? Sixteen maybe? Barely old enough to shave. But old enough to be embarrassed by a real live woman without clothes.

"Type?" Tove said.

"What?"

He stopped typing to enunciate every word, staring at the ceiling in furious embarrassment. "Can. You. Type?"

"Yes."

Tove struck some keys. "Use far edge. Please."

My chair vibrated, and a keyboard with arm rests swung up into place in my lap.

"I'll stay out of your way," I said. With two keypresses I moved my chair away from Tove's, claiming a blank section of ceiling. Another quick command, and a blank Congolese datalink rose from the armrest. I touched the datalink's screen, and it used its physical connection to retrieve my profile from the main Congolese datacore and configure itself.

I was connected again. Maybe I could do something.

First, the camera outside the door.

Palmer was on his hands and knees, panting. His head hung limp. Somehow, he'd moved a few meters until he was square in front of the elevators.

One leg twitched. His body shuddered.

That leg swiveled at the hip, scraping Palmer's knee over steel before it came up to complete the big, looping, pointless circle.

Whatever had happened to Tansi and Monard, whatever had compelled them to struggle down Spoke Five, whatever had been looping around the lights in Ring One, had hit Palmer.

No.

Whatever was *in* Tansi and Monard, whatever had traveled in the lights, it was *in* Palmer.

Some Congolese experiment, out here at the beginning of time, had created something. Maybe born from a dropped decimal point, or an inscrutably small variation between our universe and this one.

Whatever they'd made, it was in our killer cyborg.

I sent Watford a quick message. The Congolese datalink didn't have priority access to Watford, but I flagged it urgent in the hope he'd see it. *In engineering office. Palmer hit by Tansi problem.* I chewed my lip. Watford had ordered me up—but that was before Palmer's incapacitation. *Staying with him.*

There—I'd reported in, like a good flunky.

On the display, Palmer began swooping a hand over the steel deck, letting his fingers dangle like he was feeling for something. His head still hung weirdly loose.

At a gap in Tove's typing I said, "Any chance of getting the main network back?"

"Nope."

I waited for more detail. "What's going on?"

"Still trying to datacore."

It got in the lights, I thought. What if it got in the datacore?

Guessing from how the first human victims had died, there might not be much left of the datacore.

On my display, Palmer's questing fingers found something.

He thrust his hand into the deck.

A section of deck plate peeled up like putty.

I froze.

Palmer plunged his hand into the exposed opening. Bright light sparked up into his face.

Maybe we were at the bottom of Spoke Five—but Palmer could dig through the floor to get further down.

Tearing through whatever machinery was in its way.

35

Palmer's strike into the systems buried beneath the corridor floor unleashed a tumult of furious beeping.

Tove shouted, "What is that?" He actually lifted his head a few inches out of the high-gee chair, staring with a twisted snarl at the flash of red indicators on the ceiling.

I felt like screaming myself. My instincts screamed to go out and grab Palmer. Instead, I tapped the datalink. "Aidan Redding for Montague Security First Watford. Ultimate priority." Ultimate priority is relative—the actual priority depends on your role. The Congolese datalink couldn't assign Montague priorities, but I hoped that the tag would express to Watford just how badly I needed him.

I could struggle down a hallway in unnaturally high gravity. I could even climb the stairs. That only took stamina and stubbornness. Maybe an hour or two in medical.

I couldn't go up against Palmer. He wouldn't notice me attacking him.

And he'd barely notice killing me.

On the display, Palmer's shoulder worked and twisted. More sparks flew. His hand jerked up, bringing a loose chunk of cable with it.

I wanted to scream *Come on, Watford, answer me!* Instead, I said, "Deploy high-gee suit."

The chair buzzed under me. Bright blue plastic oozed out of the leg rest, up over my shins, swallowed my knees, and started climbing my thighs.

I didn't have time to pay attention to the suit. Instead, I hit another button. "Palmer! Can you hear me?"

No answer.

"He's breaking circuits!" Tove shouted.

"Tove!" I said.

"I'm losing!"

"Tove!" I shouted. "What is under us?"

"Machinery!"

I deliberately slowed my breath as I turned my chair to face him. The bright blue gee-suit had slid up over my belly, snug but not tight. It wouldn't inflate until I stood. "Tove. Listen to me."

The kid jerked his head towards me, too upset to be embarrassed by my half-naked form. "He's breaking the control cables!"

"Tove!" I said. "Before he cuts everything. What is underneath us?"

Tove scowled, but his fingers danced on his keyboard. "Conduits," he said. Palmer's image over my head shifted to the side, replaced with circuit diagrams. "Part of the Ring One neural. Datacore cell block five." The schematics flashed away, replaced with a set of graphs and gauges. "Hydrogen tank five, from scoop five." Those graphs disappeared as fast as Tove had summoned them. "Then water tank—"

"Wait!" I shouted. "That last one!"

My heart had started hammering again.

Had I seen what I thought?

Tove huffed and brought it back. "Hydrogen storage."

I swallowed.

Off to the side, a graph—and there, another one.

Jagged swoops and blocks.

Just like what I'd discovered in Tansi's and Monard's brain scans.

36

"Those graphs," I said, using my datalink to point out the chaotic, jagged spikes and blocky valleys. "Where exactly are they?"

"An error," Tove said.

"I didn't ask that!" No, too harsh. My breath wanted to come too quick, too hard. "It's important, Tove. Are those part of a diagnostic, or a system?"

"It's noise," Tove said.

I jerked my gaze to him. "Look at me, Tove."

Annoyed, he pulled his attention from the ceiling to glare at my eyes. "Busy!"

"That pattern," I said. "Everything, all of this, is about that noise. That pattern, it's why people are dying."

Tove's mouth dropped in a little O.

"If we can figure out where that pattern comes from, maybe we can stop this." I wanted to shout, but kept my voice quiet. "Tell me about it."

Tove swallowed. "Dad complained about it. It showed up a few months ago."

"When, exactly?"

Tove called up another image. "Two hundred twenty-six days ago."

I brought up the record of the earliest Congolese brain-damage victim.

Two hundred twenty-one days ago.

I licked my lips. "Where, exactly, did it show up?"

Keys clattered. "Tank Five, cell sixty-one. A few days later, cell one-sixty-four, then one-seventy-three, one—"

"How many in total?" I said.

"A couple hundred cells."

"Does it show anywhere else?"

"Not that I've seen. And Dad would have told me, he talked about it every night."

"Why here?"

"I don't know!" Tove said. "That's what was driving Dad nuts."

"What makes Tank Five special?"

Tove shrugged.

I said, more quickly, "What makes it unique? What's with Tank Five that's not on any other tank?"

On the display, arcing electricity illuminated Palmer's face. Sparks fountained past him.

"Uh, it's hooked Field Five, and Reactor Five."

"What's going on in Reactor Five?"

"Nothing!" Tove said. "Dad took it off-line, he didn't want to feed it unstable hydrogen."

"Smart man," I said. "Okay, so what makes Field Five different?"

"All the scoop fields are different," Tove said. "They're all tuned to different energy levels, different speeds."

"These are the fields that pull hydrogen out of space?"

"Yes."

"Do—"

A harsh buzz interrupted me. "Redding!" Watford said. "Answer me!"

"Redding here, sir."

"What's so urgent? And where's your datalink?"

"Palmer's digging through the floor," I said. "He's ripping up circuits."

Watford swore. "And your datalink?"

"Out with him. Decided to report—"

"Yes, yes. Any chance of getting the network back?"

"No, sir," I said, just as Tove said, "Impossible."

"Who is that?" Watford said.

"His name is Tove," I said. "Son of an engineer."

"Get a real engineer on the line."

"I am a real engineer!" Tove said.

I glanced at Tove. "Where is your dad?"

Tove swallowed. "Spoke Six."

Where the blast had happened.

No wonder Tove had been so desperate to stop that leak of corrosive smoke.

"Sir," I said. "We're it. But that's not the important thing."

"Go on," I said.

"That pattern—it's in the fuel tank under us. About two hundred cells."

"One ninety-one," Tove said.

"How did they create it?" Watford said.

"That's it, sir. They didn't. They sucked it in from outside."

"It's in the environment," Watford said.

"My question is." I licked my lips. More warning alarms snarled from the ceiling, but they were silent next to the klaxons blaring in my mind. Watford would either consider what I said, or send me back to Earth with a recommendation for eternal inspection duty.

Assuming Palmer didn't reach the tank, detonate it, and blow half of Wemm Station back into hydrogen.

"If this universe had life," I said, "what would it be made out of? What would it look like to us? And how would it feel about getting sucked into a fuel tank?"

37

"Wow," Tove said. He'd even stopped typing.

Only focused concentration me from shaking with tension. Concentration, and excess weight.

Watford held silent for an uncomfortably long time. "Stand by for orders, Redding."

"Acknowledged."

Watford had barely cut the link when I turned to Tove. "What Palmer's breaking through. Can you reroute the controls?"

"Not without network."

"Something! Get us, I don't know, some kind of backup access."

The shifting ceiling displays froze.

Tove's fingers clattered on his keyboard. "That's it." His voice sounded hopeless. "We're cut."

"Communications?" I said.

"Cut." He pounded the keyboard with the heel of his hand. "Cut, cut, cut!"

"Calm down, Tove."

"Helpless!"

"No, we're not." My words surprised me—it was like I was talking to my own reflection in a mirror. "You feel helpless—I get it, believe me. But there's always *something*. There's always a tool, always an angle, always something you've overlooked."

Tove glared at me.

"You said the magnetic shields are broken." The words made me imagine the high-intensity radiation sleeting through me, through Tove, through every inhabitant of Wemm Station. I pushed confidence into my voice, to cover up the dread. If we lived through the next few hours, we'd have plenty of time to get a chromosome scrub. "But you fixed the lube, so the station isn't breaking itself apart."

"Right. But if he—"

"Don't panic yet," I said. "Figure out where we are, first. What happens if Palmer keeps digging?"

"Bulkhead," Tove said. "Stop."

"What if he gets through the bulkhead?"

"Steel." Tove shook his head. "Structural."

"That'll stop him three minutes," I said. "Maybe four."

"What he using?" Tove said.

Is, kid. Is. "Tove. Palmer is a cyborg." Watford was going to have my head for leaking any details. "He's designed for deep space operations and construction. Palmer can bend steel with his bare hands. In vacuum. In orbit of Mercury. During a solar flare. While sipping his afternoon tea."

Despite the high-gee suit, Tove's face lost its underlying color.

I kept my voice level, projecting a calm confidence I didn't nearly feel. "So what happens when Palmer keeps going?"

Tove's hands reflexively went to the keyboard. His fingers twitched with the repressed need to call up displays. "Breaks through the cable layer—all little stuff, hydraulics and shaper stock. Then the bulkhead. I..." I saw Tove's eyes roll up as he remembered diagrams. "I think access shaft under, for robots. Hydrogen cells."

"The wiring layer." I licked my chapped lips. "What if he digs through that?"

"Everything carries on. Engineers reroute."

"Okay. The hydraulics you mentioned? Shaper stock?"

Tove waved dismissively. "Messy. Not dangerous."

When we made it through this, I was going to sign the kid up for elocution lessons.

Before I could ask the next question, Tove said, "The tank. The hydrogen tank."

"I can guess—but tell me. What happens?"

"Supercooled. Pressurized. Freeze air? Burn?"

The hastily memorized Wemm Station briefing had included information on the engineering level, but I'd concentrated on Ring Two and above. "Those tanks are large, aren't they?"

Tove nodded.

"If they burn down there—"

"Won't burn in tank," Tove said. "No oh-two. Boil up into Ring One, then burn." His face got even paler. "Burn all here."

"Then we make sure that doesn't happen," I said.

Tove hammered fists into the padded armrests of his chair, which absorbed them without complain, making him even more angry. "No controls!"

"People built Wemm Station," I said. "People like your dad, using robots and wrenches. They hung in zero gravity, in an empty universe, and built this place out of raw aluminum plates and steel beams. And somewhere underneath the datacore, every machine has actual knobs and buttons."

"Where?" Tove shouted.

I pointed at the floor. "Below us."

Tove stared at me.

I said, "Maybe that pattern down there doesn't mean anything. Maybe it's the key to everything. And maybe Ring One could handle a giant hydrogen blast. But I do know that we have a few thousand people overhead, and if Palmer rips open that tank there's a good chance that a whole bunch of them will get hurt or just flat-out die. I'm going down there, and I'm going to dump every liter of that hydrogen back out where we got it."

Tove swallowed, not saying anything.

"You don't have to help," I said. "You'd make it a whole lot easier, though."

"Never been down there," Tove said.

"Well, neither have I. But at least you'll recognize the labels on the controls when we find them."

Tove took a deep breath. "One and a half, two gee down there."

"The suits can handle that." The manual claimed they could.

Tove shook his head mutely. "That's…"

"It'll be rough," I said. "But look at it this way. Either Palmer punches into the tank and kills everyone—or we bleed off the hydrogen and save everyone."

Tove closed his eyes, looking every bit a nervous teenager.

Without even Tove's meager knowledge, I'd have to fall back on more direct ways to empty the tank. Get on a pressure suit. Take a plasma cutter outside. Climb down until I found something that looked like a hydrogen tank. And start digging.

At least the blast would be outside.

I said, "Imagine what all the girls will say."

Tove grimaced, knowing how I'd pushed his young man buttons and still unable to resist. "Fine. We do."

The comfort of the high-gravity recliner suddenly felt precious, like something I might never know again. About to leave its cradling embrace, I found part of my brain trying to absorb the pillowy sensation so I could recall it later.

We had no time for comfort.

I tapped my datalink. Even without the network backing it, it had enough brains to control the chair and my high-gee suit. "Stand up."

In one smoothly synchronized dance, the chair shifted as my suit began to inflate. After walking naked across the hall, the pressure climbing my body didn't feel so invasive. It felt—safe. Freeing.

Seconds later I was on my feet, letting the suit puff up around me. "How do we get down, Tove?"

"Access elevator," Tove said. He still lay in his high-gee recliner. Some color had returned to his face, but fresh sweat shone on his forehead.

"Where is it?"

Internal conflict battered his expression. He wanted to hide until someone rescued them. He wanted to save everyone.

But most of all, put on the spot, he didn't want to look weak or afraid.

His obvious fear made it easier for me to keep mine under control. The suit felt almost comfortable now, but that rippling squeeze that forced blood back up my legs would get a whole lot fiercer down below. Two gravities promised brutality. Not nearly as brutal as standing in Palmer's way, but still.

Tove touched his datalink. "Stand up." His voice wobbled as the chair swung and the suit compressed against him. "It's to left."

"Okay." I took a shuffling half-step towards the door before a thought struck me. "Tove, before we go."

Tove finished stepping off the chair's low foot platform. "Oui?"

"I'm from the security department. You're engineering. This is an engineering job."

Panic flashed in his eyes. "I can't go down there alone."

"No, no." I wanted to shake my head, but the suit's neck restricted that motion to a slow grind. "I'm planning to go the whole way with you." I licked my lips. "The thing is—I'm not used to high gravity."

"Neither."

"If something happens to me, if I can't finish," I said. "You *must* go down on your own."

Tove's face tried to go pale. "Dad said never."

"Blame me if you need to," I said. "But that tank's full of the same pattern that's in Palmer. I don't know if they're attracting each other or what, but we've *got* to get it out of this station."

Tove's hands rolled into the best fists the high-gee suit allowed. "Fine."

Tove was not expendable.

But I was.

Weirdly, the thought made me more comfortable.

Now to go expend myself.

38

Palmer had dug right in the center of the elevator vestibule. He'd climbed into the pit head-first, but his butt and legs were still sprawled across the deck. Bent steel flooring bloomed upwards around him. Tangled fistfuls of wire and conduit, savagely torn chunks of pipe, and smeary puddles of greasy blue and green and yellow ooze surrounded the pit. The malignant stink of a dozen different chemicals and angry electricity burned my sinuses, and Palmer's ongoing assault on the station's structure raised a cacophony of breaking metal and plastic.

The high-gee suit's rhythmic pulses up my legs, synchronized with my heartbeat, suddenly got much quicker. The suit automatically wicked my sweat away, but I was pretty sure the sight made that function work harder too.

The elevator doors across the room sat frozen, impotent. Manual controls and gauges widely spaced on the walls flashed yellow and red.

Sudden brilliant light flared up from the pit. I closed my eyes against it, but blue radiance glared against my eyelids.

Behind me, Tove swore in French.

The light faded in a second. White and yellow afterimages obscured my sight, but I started shuffling left. Not only did the suit restrict me to half steps, but I couldn't lift my feet to step over debris. The small stuff I brushed aside, but I had to painfully sidestep a half-meter chunk of copper pipe barely as big around as my arm.

The ends of the pipe had been squeezed shut. The indentations from Palmer's fingers still glowed a little red.

I tried to brush the smaller stuff aside with my toes, but quietly. Palmer's depredations made an incredible racket, but I didn't dare attract his attention.

A whiff of some noxious burnt smell made me cough—no easy feat in a high-gee suit. Fresh tears hazed my eyes. I wanted to bring up a full faceplate and respirator, but if I did, I wouldn't be able to communicate with Tove. No network meant no voice channel.

Here we were at the beginning of the universe, in the most sophisticated structure I'd ever seen, and what we needed were a couple of old-fashioned walkie-talkies.

A massive chunk of air duct sailed up out of the hole. It fell too quickly, like a video at twice normal speed. It struck well away from us, but the impact scattered fresh detritus into my path. A massive circuit board cage skittered to the side, right into my planned path. I'd have to circle it, too.

If we didn't get out of here quickly, strewn and broken components would make the vestibule impassible.

I itched to charge forward. Instead, I raised one hand in a fist and stopped. Had Tove ever seen any of those old action movies? I shuffled on my axis, needing four steps to make the quarter-turn so I could see the kid.

"Protect my eyes," I said, tapping my datalink. A clear visor flowed out of the high-gee suit's forehead and down to my nose. "You too, Tove."

Tove grimaced and followed my example.

I shuffled back to face forward.

Palmer's clattering stopped for a second, then more electronic debris hailed down around us in a fusillade of noise. Something bounced off the back of my suit, the automation thankfully reducing the impact to a faint pressure over one shoulder. In this gravity, a surprised stumble had a good chance of maiming, even killing me.

We'd scooted a yard further when the clatter stopped again. Metal groaned, a low-pitched rumble that penetrated the padded soles of my feet and shivered up my legs and into my spine. I ached to turn and look, but we needed to escape the area before the strewn scrap of station components became impassible heaps.

Palmer said, "Ing. Red. Red."

His voice sounded too loud.

Like he wasn't head-down in a pit any more.

Even inside the high-gee suit, fear tickled my skin.

"Red. Ing."

I couldn't hope that Tove's last name was also Redding.

I stopped.

The suit still refused to let me turn quickly.

Palmer sat on his knees, body straight but at a skewed angle, like a tree dragged by hurricane winds. One mad eye whirled all around. The other eye was a sphere of hot orange light, flicking with irregular, inhuman blinking. Wicked blue lightning crawled around one hand, flickering between the freckles of his sensors. His spine and shoulders jerked with each leap of light, teeth clanging together with each spasm.

Watford had said I run towards trouble.

Right now, I wanted to run away.

Instead, I took a shuffling step towards Palmer. "Tove. Keep going."

I'd expected Tove to argue. Instead, he started shuffling more quickly, his feet swinging over the ground like a tai chi practitioner's.

He knew how to move. I'd been holding him up.

Palmer's one human-looking eye didn't fix on me, but he seemed to be trying to wobble it in my general direction. "Red-d-d-d." Electronic distortion surged and distorted his voice.

"Palmer," I said. "Fight it. You can beat it."

Tove shifted past my back, just short of running.

Irrational anger flashed through me. Tove had been here before, he'd practiced in high gravity. I hadn't.

All I knew was how to stand and face Palmer.

Palmer raised the hand not covered in lightning and waved off to the side. "Fire."

I flinched. "Palmer, it's going for the hydrogen tanks. You've got to stop it."

"Fire." His voice warbled up the scale. "For, for for for—for for fire."

The lightning-sheathed hand came up, dangling a massive metal-cased block by frayed wires. The plastic coating on the wiring sizzled and smoked under the crawling blue charge. The way the whole thing swung, it had to weigh as much as I did.

"Palmer," I said, mind churning to come up with something. "Can you shut your systems down? We can get you to a medical pod before there's any more damage."

"Fire," Palmer hissed. "Firefirefirefirefire. Forfire." The arm holding the metal block swung back.

"You can stop this!" I shouted, more out of denial than any real hope.

Palmer launched the massive chunk of metal at me.

39

I instinctively lurched backwards, as quickly as the oppressive high-gee suit permitted.

As Palmer started to throw, though, his other arm swung across his body. His shoulders shifted, skewing his aim.

The chunk of metal crashed into the floor a meter to my left with a rattling thud that made me flinch.

It bounced, leaving a ten-centimeter crater in the steel deck.

With the gravity, my heart couldn't leap into my mouth—but it did grab hold of my esophagus and start climbing.

If he hit me with something like that, I was dead—adaptive suit or no.

Whatever was in Palmer had figured out that humans threatened it. Interfered with it. Maybe it had only gotten to the rock-throwing stage—but it didn't need anything more.

And it would have hit me, if that other hand hadn't interfered.

Palmer still had some control.

"Fire!" Palmer screamed. "For. For, for forfor." His hand without lightning waved frantically, while the other arm resumed those inhuman, swooping motions.

Tove had made it through the doorway and into the corridor.

So long as Palmer didn't hit the kid, Tove would solve the real problem.

All I could do was keep Palmer's attention—and not get flattened.

Palmer's shouting turned into an electronic squeal.

I took another step to the right, back towards the engineering office. "You can do it, Palmer. You can stop it. You're tougher than the rest of us."

Blue lightning surged up Palmer's arm, then ebbed back to his hand. The glowing eye flashed yellow, then incandescent white, and back to orange.

"You have to be tough," I said. "Push it out. I know you can."

Palmer's lightning hand grabbed the raised edge of a battered floor plate and tugged. The steel plate sparked, but stayed attached to the ground. Palmer tugged harder, the lightning seething furiously.

Maybe the thing in Palmer didn't understand the idea of "riveted down."

"Misdirect it," I said. "Make it wad up that floor plate instead."

"For!" Palmer screamed. "For for for!" Even through the electronic distortion, I thought I heard real anguish there.

The steel floor plate in Palmer's hand snapped.

He raised a jagged metal triangle the size of his hand over his head.

Palmer's free arm flailed wildly. Was he waving me away?

The other hand spun and hurled the makeshift shuriken right at me.

Straight into my gut.

40

The metal shard plunged in right above my left hip. My whole world seemed to focus on that point—weird hot ice, slipping straight through my skin and into my guts. Brain cells dating back to the dinosaurs screamed their outrage. I somehow tasted my own blood.

The elevator room whirled around me. Without the high-gee suit, I would have fallen.

My breath sagged out.

Primal terror filled me, certain that inhaling would shift the metal and maim me even further. My lungs held paralyzed for a second or a decade, then slowly eased air in.

The sound of my heartbeat drowned out Palmer's idiotic shriek of *for for for fire for.*

Suddenly I wasn't brave at all. I wanted to scream and run, to fall.

I wanted someone to rescue me.

I would have collapsed in shock, but the high-gee suit held me up.

The stink of burning smart fabric stung my nose.

Nausea made me want to puke.

I didn't dare.

I needed a heartbeat to work up the courage to even lower my chin and look down.

The metal jabbed out a dozen centimeters from the suit's inflated fabric, the trailing edge gleaming with hints of red heat from being broken free. My instincts itched to snatch it out of me, to pull it free—but no. Worst thing I could do.

The suit's rippling changed. It had always squeezed me in, supporting my circulation, but now it tightened around the wound.

Something jabbed my bicep.

I looked down. Nothing.

But with my next breath, the pain washed away. The suit's medical systems had fired. You can't tourniquet a gut wound, but the suit could apply direct pressure. Immobilize the injury.

And shoot me with enough painkiller to make the pain stop.

My throat hurt. I didn't remember screaming, but I must have.

I still didn't dare breathe deeply. Even without the appalling sensation, I still felt horribly aware of the injury.

But I could think.

Palmer's deranged eye wobbled in my direction. The other glared forge-red.

Every moment Palmer spent chasing me, he wasn't tearing through the Wemm Station hull. Tove needed time to blow out the hydrogen tank.

Palmer was already trying to pull another chunk of metal off the plate. I suddenly realized he'd stopped shouting, leaving me only with the sounds of humming machines and my own pulse.

I looked around desperately, trying to ignore the drugged hollowness behind my eyes. There had to be something here I could use. A big power control panel with dozens of toggles—no, if I killed the electricity down here, who knew what would happen to the station? Gauges for different kinds of liquids, fire suppression panel, conduits…

Wait.

My gaze swiveled back to the fire suppression panel: a big red button with a flip cover, a big clicky dial with a dozen settings for different kinds of fire. I didn't recall the specifics of each kind of fire suppression, but I knew that one was a simple water spray and another evacuated the air. When the datacore was online it handled fire automatically, but if a fire broke out now someone would have to choose the correct type—

Understanding hit me like a bucket of cold water.

The thought of walking filled me with dread. What if taking a step shifted that scrap of metal enough to nick an artery? The suit couldn't keep me alive if I bled out. And nobody was standing by to get me into a medical pod. The numbness in my flank seemed to be spreading—did that mean the damage was already getting worse? My heart wouldn't stop rabbiting.

But if I didn't move, many more people might die.

I took a deep breath and swung my left foot forward. The numbness in my side made me feel even more clumsy, but I planted that foot and took another step.

With careful attention I shuffled the few meters to the fire suppression panel. The knob was oversized, meant to be adjusted while wearing a high-gee suit. Each setting was numbered, and had a brief description in French.

Something metallic cracked behind me. I didn't need to turn and look to know that Palmer had snapped off another chunk of metal plate.

Moving as quickly as I dared, I twisted the dial a third of the way around and flipped the button cover.

Palmer let out a horrific electronic shriek, discordant tones twisting against each other.

I jabbed the button.

41

Even facing the elevator room wall, I saw the pale yellow mist fizzing out of the ceiling.

A noxious bitter smell brushed my nose. I jerked my hand up for protection, like my fingers could filter out gas, but the high-gee suit's smart fabric flowed up over my lips and brushed my touch away. The suit needed only a second to form a clear protective visor. A small hollow formed over my nose and mouth, feeding me tiny breaths of flat, canned air.

Behind me, metal crashed against metal.

Something clattered on the deck.

The floor thudded with a big, heavy impact.

Yellow-green condensation formed on my visor, coalescing into turgid blobs that trickled like poison rain across my view.

If I'd screwed up, if I'd made a bad assumption, another shard of metal would land right in my back. Desperate to spin, but trapped by the high-gee suit's uncomfortable clench, I needed two steps to turn around.

Palmer lay face-up, surrounded by broken equipment and shattered deck plates. The electric halo around his arm had vanished. His back arched so extremely that I felt a sympathetic ache, then he shuddered and pulled his limbs into his chest, pillbug-style.

He hadn't shouted *fire* and *for*.

He'd shouted *four*.

Palmer had told me how to shut him down.

I didn't know exactly how that particular fire suppression chemical had scrambled the construction cyborg's circuits. But at that moment, I didn't care. My pounding heart felt ready to burst. I wanted to sag against the wall, get back in the high-gee recliner, but I didn't dare. My flank felt so numb it might have been scooped out, but I couldn't forget the chunk of metal buried in me.

Drenched in putrid yellow gel, Palmer shuddered.

I took the risk of closing my eyes and concentrating on my breath, trying to slow my jackrabbit pulse and get my breath back under control. The suit's stale dry air made my mouth feel even more parched. Fading adrenaline left my muscles quivering, my stance supported only by the high-gee suit.

Were the Congolese still preparing to evacuate?

Or had Watford dispatched a team to deal with Palmer?

No, Montague didn't have the people left. He'd sent Percival and a few other people to deal with DeKalb, leaving him with just enough to guard the Portal. He'd certainly sent a message through the Portal telling the company to stand by for evacuation.

Montague wouldn't send Watford more security people until we stabilized Wemm Station… or until after the evacuation, when they brought in a science team to discover what had gone wrong.

Assuming they didn't just slam the door on this universe forever. Montague had done that more than once.

I had this sudden flash of a future life on an abandoned Wemm Station, living on stored supplies as the station slowly fell apart from lack of maintenance. Maybe I'd bring chickens down to Ring Three so I could stay near the Portal, watching for years—decades—in hope that Montague would decide to come back.

No, that wasn't going to happen. That was the painkillers talking.

Step one, talk to Watford. Tell him Palmer was shut down, that Tove was on his way to bleed out the hydrogen from Tank Five. That I had a metal triangle in my side. The main Ring One corridor had to have hard-wired communications panels, somewhere.

All I had to do was walk.

Without shifting the metal stabbing into me.

I deliberately didn't look down at my flank, tried to not imagine where exactly the weapon had wound up. Had it stuck in muscle? Or was the tip buried in my bowels? All the way through, into my liver?

Instead, I shuffled in a tight circle and headed for the nearest corridor.

The massive thud I'd heard had been the transparent firewall dropping from the ceiling, isolating the toxic goo in the elevator room from the main Ring One corridor. The built-in airlock opened at a touch, and a blast of air took the worst of the goopy fire suppressant off my suit.

I'd made it maybe a dozen meters down the corridor when I saw someone's knees and feet dropping into view from around the ring's upward curve.

42

The prospect of another brain and a set of hands sent relief surging through me. I really didn't want to deal with the damage Palmer had left as Aidan Redding versus Yet Another Universe. Seeing those feet, I didn't care if they belonged to an engineer or a Portal guard, Congolese or Montague, crew or child or knife-wielding maniac.

Although a medic would be nice.

With the hollow numbness in my side, a medic would be wonderful.

They could take over. I could take a nap.

I kept going, scanning the control-studded walls for anything that looked like a hard-wired network connection. A comms panel. I would have settled for carrier pigeons. Anything that let me call for help and get this chunk of metal out of my guts. With the suit's faceplate down, the fire suppressant's stench burned my nose. The blast of air in the firewall's airlock had blown most of it away, but that stuff was noxious enough that even the faint remnants made my stomach protest.

The other person moved much more quickly than I dared. I'd gone only a few more meters when they got close enough for me to recognize the suit's slowly shifting leopard-print decoration.

I stopped in surprise. "Habre?"

I abandoned my search and shuffled forward.

Habre saw me and somehow picked up speed, walking almost at a normal pace. The omnipresent rattle of Wemm Station's machinery almost drowned out her shout of "Redding!"

I lifted a hand.

We couldn't really speak until I was close enough to clasp the bulky glove of her high-gee suit.

Exhaustion dragged Habre's sharp features. "Redding?"

"Belvie," I said. "I am thrilled to see you." I'd heard she was dead so often, I believed it.

"What has happened? Where is everyone?"

Habre's presence boosted my spirits, but my thoughts still ground against each other like gaptoothed gears. "Have you talked to anyone?"

Habre shook her head. "I only now stabilized the survivors of the lube blowout. Where are the rescue teams?"

She'd missed everything. "Getting ready for the evacuation."

I quickly filled her in: how Palmer had attacked the floor, finding the pattern, losing communications with the upper Rings. Merely telling the story made me feel even more tired. By the time I got to where I'd disabled Palmer, I had to use my free hand to lean against the wall. The numbness around my wound had ballooned to the bottom of my ribs and down into my hips. The ache in my head made me feel tiny, as if I sat within my own skull and shifted rusty levers to move my limbs and form words.

Concerned, Habre said, "What's wrong with you?"

Not looking down, I clumsily shifted my hips a few degrees to display the jagged metal sticking out of my side. "Palmer got me."

Habre hissed. "We need to get that out of you."

"You can't." I took a deep breath. "I'll bleed out."

"No you won't," Habre said.

"The worst thing you can do for an impalement. Pull it out."

"Aidan." Habre kept her eyes on my face. "The suits are built for that."

I looked at her without comprehension.

She waved her free hand and spoke slowly. "Our high-gee suits, they have built-in medical support. You don't feel anything there, do you?"

"No."

"And you're woozy." It wasn't a question.

"You have *no* idea."

"That's the drugs and the nanomeds." Habre clearly enunciated each word, as if she was afraid I wouldn't understand. "They're standing by to patch the hole. It's not perfect, you'll need a doctor later, but it'll stop the bleeding and prevent any more damage."

The urge to yank the violating shard out of my side blossomed, tangled with an equal revulsion of anyone touching it. I'm sure Habre felt my grip clench tighter, but she only said "The nanomeds will soon exhaust their power. And when that happens, you really will bleed out."

I fumed. Montague high-gee suits didn't have anything like that. I should have known, though. I should have read the Congolese manuals, as well as the Montague ones I was still trudging through. How was I supposed to do anything without understanding the equipment, the rules?

Despite the high-gee suit's engulfing pressure and the horribly numb wound, I made myself take the deepest breath I could manage. "Okay." My flank abruptly seemed hot, a radioactive no-go zone as deadly as the storm of energy outside Wemm Station. "Give me a moment, I'll get it."

"You can't," Habre said.

I gave her a clenched-tooth grin. "You haven't seen those old cowboy movies, have you? The ones where the explorer alone does surgery on himself?"

"They were madmen," Habre said. "Listen to me, Miss Redding." Her voice took on a quiet tone. It should have annoyed me, but somehow I felt… comforted? "If anyone's that tough, it's you. But please let me help you. All you must do is stay still a moment."

I trembled. I didn't want her to touch it. *I* didn't want to touch it.

"Fine," I said. "But—quick."

"You will feel nothing until after."

I squeezed my eyes tight.

Everything held still for a breath.

In the middle of the numbness, a bright spark of warmth exploded like the first sun igniting in an empty universe. Unpleasant electric shivers rippled up my spine and down into my knees, making my muscles go slack. I slumped within the high-gee suit, held upright only by the smart fabric.

"Stop," I hissed. "Stop!"

"It's already out," Habre said.

The warmth intensified.

"Everything you feel—" Habre said.

A muscle spasm blasted the air out of me.

"—is the nanomeds," Habre said. "Don't try to fight. They're fixing you. Can you hear me, Aidan?"

"Yes," I groaned. Ghastly sensations rippled out of the wound: a crawling chill, a fresh fevered heat, tremors. "Tell me… something. Distract." I sucked a breath. "DeKalb."

"Yes," Habre said. "DeKalb." Her voice became businesslike. "I was in the Spoke Six engineering office with Ramazani and Kress, our chief engineer. For the video displays. My people and the Montague crew intercepted DeKalb." Her words lost all inflection. "I gave the order. They cut him down."

"The explosion," I said.

"DeKalb had done a lot of damage as he walked. He used the plasma cutter to sever many cables, damaged many conduits, all of them overhead. When he fell, the cutter burned into a fluid conduit." Her voice tightened. "One ruptured. That small burst ruptured three more. Weakened parts failed. A chain reaction. The corridor became… uninhabitable."

The holocaust in my side felt terrible, but not nearly as bad as Habre. She'd given an order to open fire, to kill one of her people. The other choices were worse. And more people had died. "Security gets the dirty jobs. I'm sorry."

Habre nodded, but wouldn't meet my eyes.

"You saved lives, though."

"I lost more," Habre said. "I'm just glad the fluid flow shut off."

I made myself inhale. Were the flashes of heat and cold getting weaker? "Tove shut them down, from Spoke Five."

"Tove?" Habre said. "Tove Kress?"

"I didn't know his name."

"Kress will be most proud."

"He's on his way."

"No, Kress stayed behind. Trying to stabilize the systems around Spoke Six. He said engineering teams would be joining him from above."

"No, Tove," I said. "He's on his way."

"Where to?"

The wretched spasms stopped cold. After the numbness, the sudden pressure of the high-gee suit over my side shocked me. My abs felt uncomfortably tight, just short of cramping.

Habre said, "It just finished, no?"

I nodded. Forcing my ribs against the suit's pressure, I pulled in a tentative breath and waited for the stab of pain.

The muscles on that side didn't want to stretch with my lungs. But they didn't tear. And my innards didn't complain.

The muzziness was fading from my head. The rapid withdrawal caused its own disorientation.

Habre had one hand on my shoulder. The other held an upraised twenty-centimeter long chunk of floor plate, twisted into a spiral spearhead. Blood and worse covered a third of it.

The sight made my stomach burn. "Uh… thanks."

"My pleasure."

Thin strength seeped back into my bones, without my usual reserves but enough that I no longer felt ready to collapse. The high-gee suit's support no longer felt completely necessary. Another breath cleared the lingering fuzziness in my head. "Communications," I said.

"Kress said they have failed in this half of Ring One."

"Elevators are out in Spoke Five," I said. "But I can do the stairs now."

"Then let's go."

43

"Tove," I said as we turned back towards the elevator room and the emergency stairs. For all the struggle I'd had walking while injured, Ring One's transparent firewall looked distressingly close. Yellow-green gunk obscured the view through it.

"Yes," Habre said. "You were about to say?"

"He went down to empty the hydrogen. The hydrogen with the pattern in it."

Habre frowned. "You sent Tove down for that? He's certainly not qualified."

"It was only the two of us," I said. "And someone had to hold Palmer back."

"You weren't clear, before," Habre said. "Before I addressed your injury, I fear you weren't very clear at all."

I felt certain I'd said everything—but the suit had drugged me. "Tove and I found the pattern from Tansi and Monard in a fuel tank."

Habre stopped. "What kind of fuel?"

"Hydrogen, scooped out of space. And Palmer, Tansi, Monard, everyone I've dealt with, they were all headed straight for that tank."

"You think it's attracting them?"

"Maybe. Maybe it's even alive, somehow."

"It's hydrogen," Habre said. "It can't be alive."

"I don't know," I said. "But I do know that, cut off from above, ditching everything with that pattern in it seemed like a really good idea."

Habre nodded.

"And maybe it would slow Palmer down. Distract—"

A loud clang shook the deck, hard enough to penetrate the suit's padding and send vibrations up my spine.

We both stopped. "What was that?" I said.

Habre shook her head.

The fire suppressant goo on the other side of the firewall was an even smear. From this distance, I couldn't see more chemicals pouring onto it. New fear swelled in my stomach. "The fire suppression system. If I triggered setting four… how long would that spray last?"

"Five minutes at most," she said.

The fragile trek from the engineering office and the nanomeds' assault on my innards had completely scrambled my sense of time.

But I must have triggered the flood that disabled Palmer more than five minutes ago.

Another clang rang down the hall.

"Palmer's recovered," I said. "He's busting through the station again."

<h1 style="text-align:center">44</h1>

"Quick," I said. "What's the fastest way down to the hydrogen tanks? Tank Five."

Habre looked up the corridor towards the firewall. "We have to stop him."

"We can't," I said. "There isn't a weapon on this station that can kill Palmer."

"Surely—"

I faced Habre. "Listen to me. Palmer can do deep space construction. In close solar orbit. He can break into your fusion reactors. You don't have anything that can stop him."

"You underestimate us," Habre said, anger seeping into her words. "We have cyborgs as well. There are several well-documented methods for disabling them. I know how to turn every tool on this Ring into a weapon."

At my first meeting with Watford, he'd emphasized confidentiality. If I explained Palmer's real role, he'd get me assigned to a Class D universe within the hour.

"I charted Monard and Tansi," I said quickly. "They were both going down Spoke Five. DeKalb was coming this way. Palmer, he's on the same line. They're all going straight to that signal in the hydrogen tanks."

Habre looked even more furious.

"Maybe that's what's dragging Palmer down," I said. "We need to get it off this station."

"If it's truly attracting him," Habre said, "if you bleed the fuel into space, he will just keep going."

"It'll scatter," I said. "We're spinning, it won't go in just one direction. He won't have a motherlode to home in on."

The floor shook again.

This time, with a distant bang.

Any hope I had of persuading her died with the blast's echo.

"Maybe," Habre said, glancing at the firewall. A diagonal crack spread through the clear tough plastic as she looked. "But I'm not letting your cyborg do more damage to this station."

I shook my head. "I know for a fact you can't stop him."

"Do what you wish," Habre said flatly, taking a step towards the firewall. "I will stop Palmer. Alone."

If she went through that firewall, if she approached Palmer, he would kill her.

If I went, I would die too.

Before she took a second step, I said, "Because if your gear could stop Palmer, Montague would have sent a bigger cyborg. With even fewer safety overrides."

So much for my career.

But Habre froze.

"Montague knows the specs of every device on this station," I said. "They know every piece of equipment you shipped through the Portal."

Habre turned to me, furious. "Are you telling me—"

"I'm not telling you anything you couldn't have figured out on your own," I said quickly. "Montague policy would specifically forbid me to tell you if we had a last-ditch method to protect Earth from any alien activity in this universe."

"It's empty!"

I spread my hands. "But look what's happened."

"You stopped him once!"

"He told me how."

The floor vibrated with another crash. It felt less damaging than Habre's livid glare.

"He told you?" she finally said. "Told you how to disable him?"

"Sort of," I said. "He's in better shape than the earlier victims."

"Then we ask him again."

"If he knew a better way, he would have told me." My mind scrabbled for solutions. "Can you get more of that number four fire spray down here?"

She glanced up at the tangle overhead. "I'm sure *one* of these pipes carries it."

"I'm open to other ideas," I said. "But Tove venting the fuel, it really is the best I've had. And if Palmer hits that tank, if he busts open a bunch of hydrogen into the Ring, what's going to happen?"

Habre glanced over at the firewall.

Another distant explosion.

The firewall ripped open at the crack, tumbling broad chunks of transparent plastic out towards us. A thin yellow-green haze billowed towards us.

I held my breath long enough for the suit to bring up a faceplate.

Habre coughed as the mist thinned around us. One of the lights in the ceiling had turned a brilliant red. Thanks for the warning, I thought.

"Fine," Habre said. She coughed again, the sound muffled and hollow through the suit's external speaker. Her anger still came through. "Fine. You had best be right about this."

I realized at that moment that I sincerely liked Habre.

And that saving her life had cost me her friendship.

45

Even in extreme gravity, losing the metal shard from my side made me feel fast. I concentrated on my steps, emulating Habre's quicker and looser motions. Everything in me ached to move, to run straight to our destination and send the tainted hydrogen straight out into the void. If it didn't work, at least we could move on to the next plan.

No running in high gravity. We trudged.

I still wanted to scream.

Habre kept her back to me. And it wasn't just the high-gee suit keeping her stiff.

Palmer had worked his way entirely into the floor. Every ten or twenty seconds a chunk of machinery flew up from the crater and crashed into the deck. A gust of thick yellow smoke shot up under pressure, settled heavily against the deck, and seeped back into Palmer's tunnel.

Something far below grumbled.

Brilliant light shone up the tunnel, accompanied by a whooshing sound loud enough to punch through the suit.

Habre stopped. "Amazing."

"Let's beat him down there," I said.

Habre led me to a heavy sealed door just short of the elevator room. Shattered firewall crunched underfoot. The fire suppressant goo looked like it should be slippery, but it didn't bother the suits. The door swung open heavily, exposing another airlock, this one walled in metal. The suits bulged with the quick burst of vacuum that evaporating the noxious goo from our suits, then shrank back down with repressurization. Our faceplates faded back into the suits.

Beyond, another small room with a wire-walled elevator. The main elevators were out, but this one used technology from centuries ago: a metal gate raised and lowered manually, gears and cables, a self-contained motor mounted just out of reach overhead. The elevator could hold half a dozen friendly people, or Habre and I if we stood in opposite corners.

Which she did.

The elevator began to descend through conduits, pipes, and wiring harnesses.

"If it's not the fuel," Habre said, still not looking at me. "If it's another cause. Perhaps we can divert Palmer." Her voice sounded thick with buried anger.

"Divert?" I kept my tone light.

"He wants to go down. If we can steer him to this elevator shaft instead of making his own path, it will reduce the damage he can inflict on the station. He can move down freely."

I bit back my first response: how are you going to steer him? "He'll move more quickly then."

"He will." She stared at a bright orange pipe running parallel to our descent. "Then he'll tear a hole in the bottom of the shaft."

"What's under us?"

"It goes all the way." She didn't look back at me. "You can ride this elevator to the outside of Ring One."

I swallowed.

We'd be throwing Palmer into infinity.

I did not want to kill him.

But… what else could we do?

And Habre had given the order to shoot DeKalb, when he'd been similarly affected and much less dangerous.

Could I do any less?

"Once Tove dumps the fuel." I felt even more sick. "If that doesn't work, maybe he's got some ideas on how we can move Palmer. A winch or something."

Habre nodded. She might be livid with me, with all of Montague, but we could still work together.

On this, at least.

As the elevator eased downward, my weight increased. My heart beat harder and my head felt impossibly heavy, as if my brain was truly made of concrete. The suit had been holding my jaw closed so I wouldn't accidentally bite off my tongue, but now the chin protector helped support my skull.

In the upper Rings, a couple meters of height changed your weight by a percent or two.

But down here, the further we dropped, the faster our weight increased.

The next time I visited a space station in an alien universe, I promised myself, I'm going to demand natural laws with a better way to create gravity.

The elevator ground downward in painful slowness. An access corridor rose into view and disappeared overhead. Each ratchet of the mechanism cranked my frustration even higher.

Someone had stenciled 2.0G on a wall plate. Two gravities.

The elevator rattled. I felt, rather than heard, another explosion, meters overhead and through the wall. I gripped the rail as tight as the bulky gloves permitted.

Another access space rose into view, a four-meter square with corridors running off it. Tove stood near a display wall, hands on old-fashioned mechanical dials. He slowly turned one, gaze glued to a display. Sweat drenched Tove's face and his eyes bulged. Was it just the gravity? Or had something new gone wrong?

The elevator gate clanged open, and a babble of French erupted into my ears.

We had communications.

I wanted to cheer.

Habre snapped quick instructions into the chorus. Voices quieted for a beat, then a single person answered.

My body felt draped in lead. Holding my eyelids open took concentration. With slow, deliberate care, I inched my way towards Tove. "Tove." The parched, greasy air made me want to cough, but the suit rippled so tightly that I couldn't possibly. "What's going on?"

"Arguing."

I turned down the earphones to dull Habre's argument. "Did you dump the hydrogen?"

"That's the argument."

I couldn't hope to follow Habre's rapid-fire French. Presumably she was telling the others what had happened. "Forget the signal in it—if Palmer hits that tank, the way he's doing damage, the whole thing will blow out. Drain it!"

"Arguing," Tove said. "Mvouba says, stop cyborg."

"We can't," I said. "I tried."

"Montague said."

I buried my urge to scream. "Montague said what?"

Tove tightened his lips in anger and spat out each word. "Montague Watford said you cannot stop the cyborg. You cannot turn him off. Commander Mvouba insists Montague deal with their man. You understand?"

"I'll deal with Palmer right now. Dump the fuel, that's step one."

"Mvouba says no."

I turned the earpiece back up, ready to jump in and tell the Congolese commander to give the order. Watford's voice was on the channel, though, speaking quick, fluid French. I felt a flash of surprise—I didn't know he spoke French. But Montague wouldn't have assigned Watford here if he couldn't.

I left my mike muted. "What else can we access?"

Tove gave a tiny shake of his head, not easy in the overwhelming gravity. "Engineering datacore dead. One data comm line up. Patched into control cable access hydrogen tank."

"The tank's not here?"

Tove hoisted a hand to point. "Through wall. Under cyborg."

Of course. "Can we get to the tank itself?"

"Access tunnel. Noise."

"That racket isn't normal, I take it?"

Tove shook his head.

"All right then," I said. "How would—"

I heard my name through the helmet and froze. Watford—no, he'd only mentioned me in passing, amidst a flurry of unfamiliar French. "How would we drain the tank?"

"It's all set." He pointed to a blinking square on the display wall. "Touch that, it goes."

I suddenly realized Watford had said my name again, this time in a more annoyed tone. I stopped.

"Redding!"

I unmuted my mic. "Here."

"Private channel," he thundered.

"Sir."

I touched the datalink to stop the flurry of French. "Private channel to Montague Security First Watford."

The helmet beeped. "Redding?"

"Here."

"Mvouba says that Palmer is digging through the station."

"Yes." I was too frustrated to add *sir*. "Ripping it apart with his bare hands. I slowed him down—"

"Yes, yes. Don't go into details on this network."

"We're ready to empty that tank," I said. "Get that signal out of the station." My hand twitched towards the blinking red button.

Watford's voice became stone. "You are not to do so."

46

I froze. "Excuse me?"

"This is their station, Redding. We will not be responsible for it."

"But that's—"

"I know, Redding. I agree with you. But the Congolese manage the station."

"But Palmer's wrecking it!"

"Under the influence of whatever they created."

"*Did* they create it?"

"You can't claim alien life without more evidence than a gut feeling," Watford said. "Especially not in an empty universe."

"Their scoop field dragged it in!"

"Maybe it leaked out of an upper ring."

"How far has Palmer gotten?"

"He hasn't yet hit any working sensors."

Another explosion rattled the air, this one not so distant.

I eyed the gleaming red button. "Then what?"

"If he is traveling in a straight line, he will rupture the hydrogen cells himself."

"That won't bother him."

Watford said, "The trick you used tells me that not all his systems are active. Two degrees Kelvin might shut him down."

"And if it doesn't?"

"Then the hydrogen gets leaked anyway."

"He might hit something critical on the way, or strike a spark and blow the place up!"

"Perhaps. But," and Watford's voice grew louder, "it's the Congolese's choice. Let them make it."

This wasn't merely political, this was politics gone horribly wrong. I felt ill.

"Please hold," I said.

"What was that?"

"Sorry. Please hold, *sir*." I turned to Habre, who was shouting at someone in French. I waited for her to take a breath and said, "Belvie!"

"What are you doing, Redding?" Watford said.

"Liaising." I cut the connection. "Belvie!"

Habre looked at me. The excess gravity dragged her face, making her look like anti-aging drugs had never been invented.

"It's your choice," I said.

She frowned.

"All those people yelling at each other, talking about this… they don't matter." I made my voice quiet but firm. "Watford's so frustrated with Mvouba, he's holding the whole station hostage. And Mvouba's doing the same. You're the one here, on the spot. Even Mvouba, he can't tell you what to do. You're the only one who has to live with what you choose."

Habre winced. Even through the humming machinery and from a couple meters away, I heard the shouting in her earpiece.

"Either we stand here and take what happens," I said, "or we try to save the station."

"Mvouba says this is a Montague issue, and orders me to treat it as such. *Montague* is to stop the cyborg."

"Watford's tied up in the rulebook. He will let Palmer blow out the station rather than let me act. And your boss is so mad at Watford, he would rather have part of his station explode than let Montague off the hook." Giving a shrug in two gravities is hard work. "We all have to decide. Can you live with obeying that order? Because if I knew how to stop Palmer, I would have."

Habre studied my face. "Yes." Something softened in her eyes. "You would have."

My datalink beeped. Watford.

I ignored it. "Either bleed it off, or we go try to divert Palmer. Make the call and let's move."

She glanced at the button. "You'd help with Palmer?"

Dragging my lips against the gravity, I made myself smile. "If I'm busted up in your medical bay, does that mean I get Congolese cooking?"

Habre's mouth quirked in a flash-fast grin.

I let my smile drop. "Everything in me screams to dump the hydrogen. If you say no, though, we'll go kamikaze on Palmer. But each second you wait, he's doing more damage. Cutting through more cables and pipes. Blowing up more stuff. Making it even worse."

Habre glanced at Tove's sweating face, then back at mine. "You're right."

Her eyes fixed on the blinking red button.

"Push it," I said. "Or we go fight."

Habre raised her hand—and stopped. "You believe this?"

"Completely."

"Then *you* push it."

Even without the voice channel open, I thought I could hear Watford screaming from hundreds of meters overhead.

Go against his orders?

Or let more people get hurt?

If I disobeyed Watford, my career was over.

I wanted to explore the universes.

But… how many people was I willing to kill to achieve that?

The high-gee suit didn't let me breathe very deeply. That scrap of air gasped out of me, taking my heart with it.

"Fine." I raised my hand. "It's on my head."

"Wait," Habre said.

I froze, my finger a handspan from the glowing red hydrogen release button.

"You're really going to," she said.

I didn't even try to keep incredulity and annoyance off my face. "Someone has to."

Habre nodded. "Then we do it together."

A tinny but angry babble erupted from her earpiece.

I flinched in surprise. "You've got your orders."

Habre raised a hand next to mine. "So do you."

I dragged my smile back into place. "Together, then."

We both put a finger over the button.

"Now," Habre said.

We shifted together.

Click.

Innumerable tiny lights flashed on Tove's display.

So much for my career. If I kept my job, my next assignment would be one of those Class D universes. Probably full of thorns and vinegar.

But somehow, my heart felt lighter.

"No," Tove said. "No, no, no!"

And the lightness vanished.

"What?" Habre said.

"No ack from the tank," Tove said. His hands danced over the display, making adjustments. "No, no, no!"

"Adjust it and we'll try again," I said. Tell me it's that easy. Please.

"No," Tove said. "I had tank controller before. Not now."

"Why?" Habre said.

Tove shook his head. "Line tank cut. Only way to drain, go tank."

I followed his gaze through the far wall.

The sound of another distant blast rattled through to us.

"Tell me how to drain it," I said.

"Hook console to tank controller," Tove said. "Commands."

"What are those commands?" I said.

Habre said, "He's saying it is technical. And he can't tell you how to do it."

Tove nodded.

I grimaced. "Then here's the plan. I distract Palmer. You run for this tank controller."

Even against the bloated high-gee suit, Tove's head managed to recoil an inch. His eyes widened.

"There's nobody else," I said.

"An emergency team came down Spoke Six," Habre said. "They're about ten minutes away."

"In ten minutes," I said, "Palmer might hit something vital and blow out this whole area. He might even make it to the hydrogen tank." I forced a deep breath despite the suit's pressure on my ribs. "It's like I told Belvie. What can you live with?"

Tove grimaced. "Fine! With you."

"With us," Habre said.

Her smile said we were all right. The *station* was in a universe of trouble, but she and I were all right.

47

When everything went bad in that last universe, I'd been in worse shape.

Of course, that time I hadn't needed to fend off a deranged cyborg.

Last time, I'd been bare-handed.

This time, I had a tool belt.

Maybe Palmer would hold still so I could undo his neck bolts and unmount his head.

Habre led us up the elevator and down an access shaft, to an airlock with a blinking red light by it. I raised the suit's faceplate and followed them in. The cramped airlock gave me a moment to rest.

Rest was good.

But feeling was a mistake.

The high-gee suit's rippling pressure helped push blood upward against gravity, but it did nothing to massage fluid back up into my face. After all this time down here, my mouth felt parched and eyeballs burning dry. Every single joint hurt, even between the bones of my spine. The suit's stale, almost bitter air did nothing to soothe my churning stomach.

The airlock finished cycling and opened onto a nightmare.

The areas behind us had only seemed like jumbles of equipment. Here, monstrous pipes ran every which way. Thick bundles of multicolored wires wound around the steel skeleton anchoring everything. Every device, every pipe, bore a stenciled alphanumeric label. Pinpoint lights were stuffed in almost randomly, wherever they'd fit, casting irregular distorted shadows everywhere. I saw no wall other than the one we came through, no floor, no ceiling: everywhere, only more machines.

Somewhere above and ahead, metal crashed.

Palmer was still at it.

Even without the thick yellow smoke everywhere, the space would have been disorienting. The billowing haze made the lights flicker as it sank, fogging everything. It was so thick, I thought I should be able to taste it. Tiny yellow droplets condensed on my visor.

"Tove," Habre said. "Will our suits handle this smoke?"

"Don't know." His voice sounded even more strained.

"Then hurry. Where is this tank controller?"

Tove's helmeted head swiveled. "There, think."

I wanted to shout that he better be certain, not think. It wouldn't help. Tove wasn't a kid, but he wasn't old enough to be leading us.

Tove was the best option we had.

We lumbered along a narrow catwalk of crisscross metal web. Lights shone up through the diamond-shaped gaps, burning yellow through the haze. Another crash, louder than the last, should have made me jump, but I weighed far too much for that.

We dragged ourselves another ten meters or so before Tove said, "Yes! This."

Beneath us, a massive array of silver tanks sat webbed in wiring. Thin silver tubes coiled around each tank like metal pythons squeezing their prey. A ladder, surrounded by a safety cage, ran up into the machinery, down to the side of the tanks, and disappeared into the impossibly thick yellow mist.

Who was going to climb a ladder in two gravities?

"Go," Habre said.

I couldn't see Tove's face, but I saw the flicker of hesitation in his stance. After a heartbeat he grabbed the edge of the ladder, swung a foot out over the edge, and started down.

"How is he doing that?" I said.

"The suit does the climbing," Habre said. "He only needs to ride."

Another clatter erupted above us. This time, the noise continued, growing louder, even echoing in this weirdly tangled space.

I glanced up.

Something shifted and moved through the haze. Something long. Turning.

Realization hit me barely in time for me to shout "Look out!"

Habre was already moving.

Three meters of battered steel pipe fell nose-first right between us. One end struck the walkway and ricocheted back up, with a ring like a giant's bell.

I instinctively threw myself backwards, trying to bounce out from beneath it. The suit caught my first step, though, refusing to let me overbalance. One hand grabbed the railing. I threw the other one up to cover my face.

The pipe came down.

Hard.

It struck right below my wrist.

Something inside my forearm went *snap*.

A wave of nauseous vertigo flooded through me.

The pipe slid off me, clattered to the catwalk, rolled towards the edge, caught on a tangled wiring harness, and rocked to a halt.

I instinctively wanted to grab my hurt arm with the other hand. I gripped the rail instead, feeling ready to collapse.

I tried to bring the broken arm to my chest. The motion made bone grind sickeningly against bone.

Another clatter from above.

I didn't want to move.

I looked up anyway.

Even through the nasty yellow haze, through the waves of pain from my arm, through two or three tangled layers of wiring and machinery, I glimpsed Palmer's glowing eye scant meters above us, backlit by fires burning far overhead.

48

"Redding!" Habre shouted.

"Arm broken," I gasped.

Habre glanced up towards Palmer, then down towards Tove. "Watch him. I'm going up."

I focused on Habre. "You can't stop him."

Habre crouched with her knees, keeping her back straight, and grabbed the pipe. "We have to slow him down. And you can't climb with a broken arm."

The suit pricked me again. The pain in my arm stopped like its power had been cut. Any moment, I'd start to feel woozy.

"How quick will the nanomeds help?" I said.

"If they haven't started, you probably don't have any left," Habre said, raising the pipe to vertical like a flagpole.

So the Congolese miracle suits had limits.

Really inconvenient ones.

I bit back a bitter remark. "Go," I said. "If he gets through you, he won't get through me."

I saw a quick flash of teeth behind Habre's visor—a smile? She stuck the pipe to the back of her suit, where it clung, and started climbing.

I ached to climb up right behind her—or, better still, in front. Instead, I hugged the elbow of my broken arm to my chest and peered down. "Tove, how are you doing?"

"Not talking," he shouted back.

"He's coming, hurry up!"

The screech of bending steel from overhead made me wince.

Tove spat out single words. "It. Is. Not. Talking!"

I wanted to scream, but held my voice steady. "Tove, you can do this. You know what you're doing."

I desperately hoped I wasn't lying to him.

Looking up, I couldn't see Palmer's eye any more. The yellow haze obscured everything, but I thought I saw something wiggling. An arm, maybe? I'd seen his eye—was he climbing down head first? In almost two gravities?

"Come on, Habre." I leaned over the ladder to look at Tove, only a couple meters beneath me. "Go back to basics, Tove."

"Fine!" Tove snarled. "Ninety-six hundred, eight en one!"

"What?" I said.

"Answering!" he shouted. "Slow, but—yes!"

"Dump it!" I shouted.

"Trying! Slow!"

Overhead, metal rattled. A long narrow shape slid into view—Habre's pipe? She'd shoved the pipe in Palmer's way, adding another barrier.

Habre shouted something indistinct.

Maybe we could stuff Palmer's debris in his path quickly enough.

Through the gap, I saw Palmer's thrashing arm.

Crawling electricity erupted over his hand.

Habre screamed.

I wrenched to look up.

Her suited form tumbled down the ladder cage towards me.

I pulled my head back just in time for her leg to fall into reach. If she'd fallen freely I couldn't have dodged, but she bounced bonelessly around the circular safety cage. How could she be that limp?

I grabbed her leg, desperately hoping to keep her from falling all the way down to Tove.

The previously plump suit sagged at my touch, letting me easily grab a handful. Habre might as well have been wearing a clown's ridiculously oversized pants.

I didn't stop to question my luck, but yanked as fiercely as I could with my one working arm, yanking her leg back onto the catwalk.

Habre's butt hit the edge of the catwalk. I dropped the leg and snatched at her chest, trying to pull the rest of her to safety. One hard yank, and Habre rolled forward, toppling onto her side in an L shape. The entire high-gee suit hung slack around her. I couldn't see anything behind the faceplate.

My pulse thudded in my temples. *Please don't be dead, Habre.*

Palmer's electric field had killed her suit. How did the airflow work? Was she suffocating already?

She wasn't grabbing at her faceplate.

Lying on her side, in two gravities—did she have the strength?

No, even in that gravity, she would move. She'd drag her hands to her face and grab for air.

If she was awake.

I could grab her. Tell my datalink to use my suit's smart fabric to form a hose and feed her oxygen. I couldn't let her survive the fall and then smother.

Before I could move, two tightly spaced metal pipes over my head screeched.

Palmer's lightning-wreathed hand thrust into the open air above me.

49

"Tove!" I shouted.

"Soon!" he screamed.

"Sooner!"

Palmer's hand still moved in those bizarre circles. He didn't use leverage to bend the pipes, instead using windmilling strikes to batter them centimeter by centimeter out of his path.

I had nothing that could stop him.

"Palmer!" I shouted. "Palmer, can you hear me?"

Once he squeezed between those final pipes, only the thin catwalk blocked him from Tove and the hydrogen tanks.

And my flimsy self.

Think, Redding! Think!

When he got through the pipes and fell to the catwalk, maybe I could grab him. Push him over the far edge of the catwalk. He'd either keep going down, or he'd turn and go straight at the tank.

If he went for the tank, he'd only need a minute.

Palmer had withstood the mind-destroying pattern better than anyone. Was it because he was half machine? Did he have some special personality characteristic? Was he just tougher and meaner than the others?

No, each victim had been successively less damaged. Palmer just had the terrible luck to catch it next.

Another hand thrust between the pipes. This hand flailed erratically, back and forth rather than around and around.

Sudden inspiration made my stomach drop out of me.

Each victim was less damaged than the one before.

The pattern had jumped from DeKalb to Palmer.

If I could make it jump into me…

I didn't want to think about that.

The pipes creaked further apart.

I didn't have any better ideas.

How had it transmitted into Palmer? His finger—he'd plugged into the network with a finger. A finger on the hand sheathed in crawling lightning.

I fumbled at my tool belt. I had to have something that would conduct a signal. Wire cutters, wire strippers, wire solder—not a scrap of wire.

That left bare skin. I'd have to retract the suit glove. I'd probably need to override safeties, what with the toxic yellow whatever-it-was.

Palmer's glowing eye appeared behind his arms.

Habre's unmoving body lay at my feet.

I couldn't save her.

But I could keep her from dying uselessly.

If I kept Palmer from breaching those tanks, if I kept a massive explosion from blasting through Ring One and wrecking the station and killing how many people, it'd be worth frying my own brain.

If I only became half as damaged as Palmer, maybe they'd let me feed myself.

With a spoon.

I didn't know if this would work.

The idea that it might terrified me.

But not trying would feel worse.

And if that tank blew, Tove and Habre and I were dead anyway.

Maybe Tove would say nice things about me.

"Palmer!" I shouted. "I think it's alive, somehow!"

The flailing arm caught the electricity-wreathed looping arm, trapping it against the pipe. Sparks flew. The electrical halo faded.

Earlier, Palmer had used one arm to throw the other off balance. To try to make the throws miss.

Something of him was still in there.

"Palmer!" I said. "I'm going to grab you. Try to—to, push it into me."

The trapped arm spun itself free.

"It might even be intelligent!" I shouted. "Maybe you can communicate, somehow. Tell it to go for me!"

Even if the derangement affected me as badly as Palmer, I was less dangerous.

Tove would have a few vital moments to flush the tank.

Even if I got down, even if I killed Tove doing it, we wouldn't destroy the station.

My chest felt even tighter than the high-gee suit made it.

Let's see Watford write me up after this.

"Tell it to leave!" I shouted. "Push it out!"

Palmer's body weaseled a few centimeters further down. His battered, filthy head squirmed into view. He looked like he'd lost an argument with the All-Star Ball Peen Hammer Team.

Once again, Palmer's one arm trapped the other against a pipe.

Sparks curled around his grip.

If I reached up, I could almost touch him.

No point in opening my suit yet.

Hopefully that yellow haze wouldn't melt my hand right off.

But which hand should I expose? The numb one? Would broken nerves interfere?

A tangle of tension, fear, and just a little hope made me quiver.

If this failed, if the yellow smoke killed me on contact or Palmer fried my nervous system, I'd never know.

If this worked… I'd probably never know either.

"Almost!" Tove shouted.

Palmer slid down another centimeter.

Almost low enough.

My mom and dad had thought I belonged in the barrio. Dad had commanded me to try to live on the universal stipend, or get a degree in the arts. Mom hid tears each time I got a little closer to working for Montague.

But I'd insisted.

And even now, I didn't really regret it.

I'd had better hopes, that was all.

Even with all my parents' arguments… right now, I had a bone-deep longing to see them again.

Palmer again caught the looping arm with the other. "Red…"

Worse, that last peaceful conversation with Habre flashed back to me. Maybe I didn't want a family now… but one day? Maybe?

If they could put my brain back together, maybe I'd still have that chance.

"Communicate!" I shouted. "Push it out! Tell it to go!"

The looping arm yanked. His other arm slid down, but he managed to catch onto the other wrist.

I had to believe that Palmer controlled that one arm. That he was trying to help me.

Help me drain whatever it was out of him, and into me.

I raised my good arm. "Another couple centimeters," I said. "Tove!"

"Almost!"

"I've got seconds!"

Maybe I'd only burn off my hand. Nobody could say I didn't try.

I lowered my hand to tap my datalink. "Retract right glove."

The words ENVIRONMENT CONTRAINDICATED scrolled across the bottom of my faceplate.

"Override safeties," I said.

The words flashed red and disappeared.

Oven heat brushed my fingertips and started crawling towards my wrist. My skin didn't fall off. The nerves didn't detonate and die.

The heat quickly became painful, though. I wanted to grit my teeth, but the suit already held my mouth closed, so I settled for panting.

I raised my ridiculously heavy, exposed hand towards Palmer's.

Even through the haze, I saw the back of my hand quickly turning red.

The good thing was, this shouldn't take long.

"Tove!" I said.

"Command load!"

My fingers brushed air just short of Palmer's outstretched arm.

Palmer spasmed.

I took an involuntary step back as he crashed both arms into a duct.

The motion brought him down that last, vital bit.

My hand really hurt now, needles of heat digging towards bone. "Hold still!"

The fully possessed arm began another loop. Palmer kept a death grip on the wrist, though. I held my fingers upraised, ready to catch him when he went past.

Just before I could, though, he crashed the haunted arm back into the duct—once, twice.

"Stop that!" I shouted.

"What?" Tove bellowed.

"Not you, Palmer!"

This exchange had let Palmer's arm begin another loop, just out of my reach.

I hissed a breath through my teeth and crouched just a little, as if I could leap up against the nightmare gravity. My poor hand felt like I'd doused it in alcohol and lit it as a torch. The muscles of my raised arm ached from being hoisted, and I couldn't even use the other to help support it.

Maybe I should break a few more bones before trying to suck in this thing. Give it a *truly* crippled host.

No, if I somehow lived, I'd never live that one down.

I straightened.

Palmer's hands came almost within reach.

I stretched.

He smashed both into the same abused duct again: *crash—crash—crash.*

A twitch pulled through Palmer's entire body.

I pulled my inflamed hand back down, fighting the urge to stick it beneath my armpit or in my mouth to cool it. One strike, then two, then three. What was he doing?

Hanging like a butterfly trying to wriggle free of its cocoon, he spasmed.

The dangling arms thrashed. Palmer lost his grip.

Then Palmer's head wrenched forward, crashing into one of the pipes he struggled to escape.

Crack—crack—crack—crack.

Four.

Wait—was he—

He'd counted one, two, three.

Was the thing in him answering with a four?

My mouth wanted to hang open.

Palmer grabbed his own arm and slammed it against the duct.

Five times.

The abused ductwork sagged and broke away, bouncing off the handrail and clanging and bouncing into the invisibly hazy depths.

I couldn't help flinching as his head battered the pipe in response.

Six times.

Palmer hung unmoving.

Excitement bubbled up in me. "Is it answering?"

"Yes!" Tove shouted. "Any second!"

"Not you! Palmer!"

Palmer's only response was methodically smashing his arm into another conduit, seven times.

"Yes!" Tove shouted. "We're bleeding pressure! Emergency flush, all cells!"

Wincing, I dragged my roasted hand back to the datalink. I didn't feel the plastic, but heard the beep. "Restore suit integrity."

I saw, but didn't feel, the smart fabric flow over the hand.

No shot of painkiller, though.

My heartbeat seemed to stammer in my veins. I'd almost tried to cook my own brain, and had only cooked a hand. And Palmer had established a brutal communication with the thing inside him.

It was alive.

It was intelligent.

Not much communication. Nothing beyond *are you there?*

But enough to slow him down.

But had I been right on the pattern?

"Half empty!" Tove shouted.

Palmer hung still as a sleeping bat.

His head twitched, as if to strike the pipe again.

"Drained!" Tove shouted. "Empty!"

I sagged inside the suit, watching Palmer.

The cyborg twitched. Shuddered. A spasm rippled up him, then another. Electricity reignited around his hand.

I stepped back. He could kick the empty tank all day long, as far as I cared. I couldn't stop him. He could even punch a way out through the outer hull and launch himself into space.

I never thought Palmer would be the one to win the award for Most Likely to Confuse Archaeologists in Thirteen Billion Years.

But it was his if he wanted it.

The electrical sheath surged.

Then Palmer sagged.

His limp body, still wearing that ridiculous mesh, slid between the pipes and dropped heavily to the catwalk to sprawl face-up. The crash of his impact was the quietest noise he'd made since this started.

He didn't move.

I blinked.

Somewhere in all this mayhem, he'd lost the banana hammock. It's not that I was looking, but he was all splayed out there.

The poor guy didn't have *anything* beneath it.

Dammed lakes of exhaustion broke free and flooded through me. "Tove," I said. "Tove, you did it. He's stopped."

I couldn't do anything for Palmer. I had no idea where to start. Instead, I made my way over to Habre. Using an elbow on the handrail for support, I managed to kneel beside her.

The suit still looked deflated. I couldn't see through the yellow-streaked faceplate. Under that broken smart fabric, Habre might be charcoal.

I lowered the broken arm to her chin and used the cooked hand to tap the datalink. "Emergency air supply to damaged suit."

I sat there the whole time Tove went to lead the emergency team in.

For right now, this was officially Not My Problem.

50

"I can't decide if I should give you a commendation or the most negative report I've ever filed," Watford said.

The reduced gravity of Watford's spartan office felt luxurious. A comfortable splint on my arm and half a mummy's worth of blissfully numbing trauma patches on the roasted hand made it even better.

I'd just had that hand regrown, damn it.

But I was clean.

Soap was humanity's greatest invention.

No, painkillers. Painkillers were the greatest.

If I ever got a nap—even a short nap, like sixteen hours, that would be better still.

I didn't have the energy to argue with Watford. So I didn't say anything.

Watford's face burned bright red. "You as good as told Habre that Palmer was here as our big hammer. You joined her in trying to dump the fuel. And you threw yourself into danger. Without training. Again."

I worked my mouth. Even my jaw joint ached. Speaking felt like too much work.

Watford continued, "We gave you a chance with this assignment. Part of a managerial role, even low-ranking ones, is to make sure you can solve problems and maintain confidentiality. Well?"

I made my mouth work. "Sir. Yes, sir."

"And why did you do that?"

I made myself take a wonderful, unconstrained, deep breath. The combination of exhaustion and painkillers felt liberating. I felt no obligation to tidy up the truth. "Because I wasn't going to let Habre die. I wasn't going to let part of Wemm Station blow out. I wasn't going to let them call evacuation. Not if I could do anything to stop it."

"Right." His eyes jerked. "Don't you dare go to sleep on me, Redding."

"Sir, yes," I yawned, "sir."

"We lost four people today."

I woke right up. *Percival.* "Yes, sir."

"Someone has to pay for that. And you are the worst political officer I've ever had. The *worst*." Watford took his own deep breath. "Montague has many security positions that are more suited to your talents, however. Not to mention your insane luck."

I made myself sit up straighter. Maybe that'd help me stay awake. "Luck, sir?"

"We have Palmer wired up."

"Is he okay?"

"He'll be fine. We're shipping him back to Earth for a full rebuild."

"But…"

"Yes, Redding?"

"The thing in him, it bashed his head. Hard. Over and over. I know he's got protections up there, but still—doesn't he have a concussion? Or something?"

Watford rolled his eyes. "Palmer doesn't keep his brain in his head, Redding."

"Oh."

"And it's not in his rear, either, so don't make that joke. No, he told me you suggested communicating. The numbers back and forth slowed it down long enough to bleed out the hydrogen tank."

I leaned forward, interested despite the painkillers and fatigue. "And?"

"He felt it leave his body. No—he felt it *decide* to leave his body."

I leaned back against the chill, hard, metal seat. It felt wonderful. "So it was intelligent."

"You had a lucky guess. Don't think it was anything but. The Congolese might have invented something here, but they wouldn't have created a mind without knowing it." Watford frowned. "Or maybe they did. It'll keep their researchers busy, along with their repair crews."

"Sir." It seemed a safe answer.

"So, do I send you to Human Resources with a positive report, or a negative one?"

I shook my head. "Whichever you think best."

"You really don't care, do you?"

"I'm too tired to care, sir. But…" I licked my lips. "I was ready to die to protect these people. I am not a political person. But that's a job I'll do."

Watford studied me. "Palmer also told us your insane idea of taking that thing into yourself."

I held silent.

His lips tightened. "No matter what, you're worth more alive than dead. Remember that. The sad thing is—if Palmer hadn't delayed it a few seconds, transferring it would have been worth a try. You're a lot less dangerous than Palmer."

I wasn't sure what to make of that. "Yes, sir."

"Hmmpfh." He put his arms on the metal desk. "Here it is. You're on medical leave. The Portal's crowded right now, we're still bringing emergency Congolese crew through. We've got an extra dozen Montague folks on Portal duty, everyone we can fit in the chamber, but they're still overloaded. As soon as we have a gap in the schedule, you're going back to Earth. Probably tomorrow, or the next day. And of course, I'll be filling out a report, as per regulations."

Here it came. "Sir."

"I'm recommending you for remedial political and administrative education."

Tired as I felt, I still flinched. "Sir."

"I'm also recommending you for advanced security training." I opened my mouth to speak but he cut me off. "You're clearly going to go in for trouble. Tritium mine guard isn't the right place for you—though you'll have to take your turn at that grunt work, same as everyone. Montague needs to put you in something like Retrieval. Maybe even Disaster Intervention."

I blinked. "Sir?"

"It takes years to get there." He tightened his lips. "I did Disaster for a few years. If you decide to go for that, and if—*if!*—you keep your nose clean for the next few years, let me know. I might write you a recommendation. But you must learn the administrative stuff. To keep your mouth shut. You *must.*"

I made myself sit up straight again. You had to be good to go into Disaster Intervention—crazy good. And a little crazy. "Sir, I don't know…"

"You don't know anything, you're stupid tired." Watford sighed. "Get out of my sight. I'll let you know when the Portal has a time slot for you."

I stood "Sir."

"Go on. Git."

I heaved myself to my feet. My knee and hip joints still burned from high gravity, and my back felt full of corrosion. I'd taken two steps towards the door before a thought struck me. "Sir?"

Watford sighed. "Yes, Redding?"

"As I'm on medical discharge… and I have to have full medical and nanomed purge anyway… I'd like to have a meal with Habre." He opened his mouth to respond, but I plowed on. "It might be good for relations, might help my successor. Sir."

He frowned. "Can she even eat right now?"

"It's the principle, sir."

Watford's frown graduated to a scowl. "You do *not* tell any other Montague people about this. I'd have a full-on revolution up here."

I smiled. "Sir."

I trudged off to bed, wondering what universe I'd see next.

Epilogue

Triumph.
Almost.
Many saved from mad space. Many destroyed trying to rescue them.
New ideas, though. Strange new ideas.
Most bizarre: solid.
Solid *means danger.*
Normal space hints at solid: *bits of life that stuck together. Became heavy.*
Spread the knowledge of solid.
Study solid.
That huge bulge of solid *that destroyed so many? Too much. Avoid.*
But little solid, *everywhere else?*
Break them up.
Make sure no solid *here.*
No solid *ever.*
Protect everyone.

About the Author

https://mwl.io

Never miss another new release!
Sign up for Michael Warren Lucas' mailing list at
http://mwl.io.

the Montague Portal series
No More Lonesome Blue Rings
Sticky Supersaturation
Forever Falls
Hydrogen Sleets